SALVAGE TROUBLE

MISSION 1

BLACK OCEAN: GALAXY OUTLAWS

J.S. MORIN

MAGICAL SCRIVENER PRESS

Magical Scrivener Press
www.magicalscrivener.com

Publisher's Note: This is a work of fiction. Names, characters, places, and incidents are a product of the author's imagination. Locales and public names are sometimes used for atmospheric purposes. Any resemblance to actual people, living or dead, or to businesses, companies, events, institutions, or locales is completely coincidental.

Ordering Information: Special discounts are available on quantity purchases by corporations, associations, and others. For details, contact the publisher at the address above.

J.S. Morin — First Edition

ISBN: 978-1-939233-38-7

Printed in the United States of America

SALVAGE TROUBLE
MISSION 1

THERE WAS something unsettling about being inside a dead ship. Darkness filled corridors where emergency lighting should have glowed. Anything to be seen existed within the claustrophobic radius of the hand lamps. Bare steel corridors devoid of air snaked their way through the inert hulk. Mag-boots snapped against the floor at each step, the pull to break them free keeping the pace slow, but safe.

It could have been worse. With a ship dead in the Ocean, sometimes they lost gravity as well, but whatever wizard set the ship's internal gravity had done a better job of hardening it than the engineers who built the onboard systems had. The mag-boots were just a precaution for all the places where the passenger freighter had been blasted open to space; without them, Carl and his crew could still have walked against the floor—but also might get thrown out into the void if something structural gave way.

"Got another one," Chip's voice came over the comm, popping and crackling with static. The voice filled the EV suit helmet and was starting to give Carl a headache. "Gimme a hand."

Carl backtracked and found Chip with one of the door panels pried open and a tangle of wires hooked to a handheld power supply. With the lock powered open, the two men were able to manhandle the door. Inside, a bunk and a footlocker were wedged into a ragged hole in the wall with the stars showing beyond.

"Must've lost everything else when the hull failed," said Carl. Fortunately his own voice merely echoed within the shell of his helmet.

Chip stomped into the room—he couldn't help stomping with mag-boots on—and gave the footlocker a tug. It fell from the hole and slammed to the floor. There was something Carl never could wrap his head around—the silence in vacuum. He felt the little tremor in the deck plates, but that was it. Chip struggled and dragged the footlocker to the door.

"I'm gonna pop a gut moving this thing," said Chip. "Can't we just get Mort over here and kill the gravity?"

"Can you even picture Mort in an EV suit?"

"Naw, guess not. Wouldn't want the cranky old bastard along anyway," said Chip. "He'd manage to find some way to make this corpse a bigger hazard than it already is."

Tanny's voice popped over the comm. "You know this is an open channel. Mort can hear you."

"Dammit," said Carl. "He's not in the cockpit with you? Get him the hell out of there before we have to—"

"Relax," Tanny said, her voice calm and measured. "I'm down in the galley making some lunch. I keyed the comm to ship-wide. Mort's right here, eating a sandwich. Want to say anything to him?"

"Um, sorry, Mort?" Chip said. "You're not a cranky old bastard? Except that you are and you damn well know it."

"Can you all shut up?" Mriy interrupted. Her voice was

scratchy even without the interference over the comm. "The sooner we finish, the sooner we eat."

"Beer's on me," Roddy's high-pitched voice agreed. "I'm not seeing anything worth salvaging among the mechanicals. Ship was unarmed; engines are slag. Computers might have seen an EMP, might not have; I'll let Chip figure that out back home. We've already cut them out and made a trip back with them."

"Hear that, Tanny?" Carl asked. "We're hard at work over here while you're chowing down bacon cubes. Grab something quick and get back to the cockpit. We've got an asteroid coming in a couple hours and I want someone watching for it. I got better things to do than become a decorative splotch on a space rock."

"Two hours, four minutes, thirty-one seconds. I've got a timer set. Twenty minutes out, you're either back on board or I leave without you. And I'm having the chicken cubes. The bacon's three months past expiration."

"You wouldn't," Carl replied. "And the bacon's fine. Those dates are just rules and regs. Total bullshit."

"Yeah, the bacon's fine," Chip agreed.

"I don't see what you find so appealing in that dry, bloodless meat," said Mriy.

Carl waved his arms for quiet, even though Chip was the only one who could see him. "Wait, wait, wait. First, bacon is humanity's crowning achievement in food. Second, you're not leaving without us. Mort would never let you get away with it."

"Mort's always liked me better than you," Tanny replied. Carl could picture the smirk on her face without needing to see it.

"Everyone likes you better than me," said Carl. "That doesn't mean he's going to let you strand us here to get dusted. Besides, you can't just take my ship."

"I'm still listed as your next of kin."

"Fuck." Carl just mouthed the word, not wanting to admit

over the comm that she was right. Sometimes avoiding paperwork caused the most inconvenient problems. "Fine, but give us until ten before the asteroid."

"Twenty."

"Fifteen?"

"Twenty."

"OK, twenty. Give us a heads up at ten and five before then, so we're not caught with our pants down."

"The *hell* are you doing over there?" Tanny asked.

"Is there atmo in your section?" Roddy asked. "What are you and Chip—?"

"Nothing!" Carl snapped. "Just, everyone get back to work. And thanks for the extra time over here, sweetie."

"You *don't* get to call me that anymore!" A thump over the comm cut out halfway through as someone switched hers off with a fist.

"School drama's over, kiddies. Back to work."

"Yes, sir," Mriy and Chip answered in discordant unison. Carl didn't need to hear Roddy's reply. He would just get back to work. Roddy was good like that.

They went door to door, overriding locks where they could and going through with plasma torches where they could not. The salvage team kept in contact, giving a running account of the dregs left behind when the survivors abandoned ship. Standard issue footlockers with standard issue locks—some weighed more than others, but none was heavy enough to be stacked with gold or any other form of hard currency. It was like visiting relatives off-world for Christmas, except the presents were a uniform matte stainless steel. No one knew you well enough to get you what you really wanted, so what you ended up with was a crap-shoot of ill-fitting clothes and knickknacks that would get tossed in a corner or sold off the first chance you got. Best case, there might be magic in one of those knickknacks, but there was no way to tell until Mort had a look. Odds ran against finding anything enchanted though, since the passengers had abandoned ship—most magic was worth the space in an escape pod.

Carl was panting, fogging the bottom half of his helmet's mask with each breath before the recirculator cleared the moisture. His back was aching from dragging plunder back to the *Mobius*. Thirty-two was too young to have an old man's body, creaking and protesting after a few hours of manual labor.

"That's it," Carl said over the comm. "No more holovids until I get back in fighting shape. How long have we got left?"

Tanny's voice squished and chomped. "Just over half an hour until the asteroid makes a sweating, scruffy paste out of you." The sound of her chewing made Carl's stomach grumble.

Roddy's comm opened. "I didn't know you navy boys even *had* a fighting shape. 'Fits in the seat, fit enough,' right? *Eee, eee, eee.*" Carl gritted his teeth.

"Captain!" Chip's use of his honorary title caught his attention. It meant someone was taking things seriously. "There's a pod jammed over here."

"Hey now! There's a bit of a break. Bulky, but portable if we can get it out of the ship's gravity. Nice work."

"There's *people* in it!"

"Of course there's people in it. You don't eject an empty—oh shit! We've gotta get them out of there quick."

"On it!" Chip replied.

"Mriy, Roddy, get back to the *Mobius*. Ready a winch and tethers for full EV. Me and Chip'll take care of things from inside."

"But Captain, we just spent five minutes cutting into the med bay—" Mriy whined.

"Anything not in your hands or your packs now, leave it! We can make another run in if there's time." Carl knew there would be no time to spare.

Carl flipped off the switch for his mag-boots and ran down the corridor, hand lamp creating a jiggling spotlight along his path. They had been on the ship for hours, and he had an idea where the hull was open to space and what sections were largely intact. He rounded a corner and found the wall of escape pod cradles, the safety doors all closed in a neat line, keeping the ship safe from the vacuum left when the pods were launched. Chip had already cut the hinges off one of the doors. He stood bent awkwardly over where it lay on the deck, the stance of a man whose mag-boots were stuck where he last set them and had neither the time nor inclination to move them. The bright flare of the plasma torch in his hand bit into the docking clamps that secured the pod to the ship.

"What've we got in there?" Carl asked, hanging back far enough to keep out of Chip's way. Two could work side by side with plasma cutters, but most times just got each other's elbows to the ribs.

"Locking clamp didn't release. Probably software, but it's quicker cutting than debugging it."

"Inside. I mean inside."

"Woman and a boy. Saw them waving from the window. Shit, if I'd have been looking the wrong way, we'd have left them here and never known it."

Carl peered through the entry hatch window. "Don't see them in there."

"I think I got across that they needed to belt in. Who knows if the grav in there is any good? They might be on ship's—"

Chip's next words were lost when a jet of compressed gas burst from a ruptured line. It looked like nothing more than an aerosol spray, scaled up to a size that would send an escape pod clear of a doomed vessel. As the pod snapped free of the half-cut docking clamp, Chip was bent over backward by the blast until his mag-boots came free of the deck. He slammed into the far wall of the corridor head first and slumped to the floor in a heap, the lit plasma torch burning into his leg with no reaction. The only sound had been a *thump* heard through Chip's open comm.

"Chip!"

"What happened?" Tanny shouted into the comm.

Carl rushed to Chip's side, pulled the plasma torch from his hand, and shut it off. "Chip took a blast from a launch jet." The EV suit had sealed around the skin where the torch had burned, keeping it from losing air pressure. It was a good sign. He looked to the life support panel on the chest of Chip's suit, and the heart rate and respiration indicators were reading zero. Damaged in the blast? No, they would have been dark; they had a reading on Chip and the reading said he was meat. "No pulse, no breathing."

"I'll double back to the med bay and—" Mriy growled into her comm. She always sounded angry when she was nervous.

"No." Captain felt around under the back of Chip's helmet, below the base of the skull.

"But captain—"

"His neck. Nothing in the med bay's gonna help him."

"Oh God, Carl," said Tanny, her voice choking off in a sob before the comm closed.

Carl's own vision blurred as he looked down at Chip's body. He blinked away the saline build-up, unable to wipe it away from behind his helm. "Get that pod on board the *Mobius*. I'll get Chip out with me."

Whatever treasures the last pair footlocker might have held, Carl would never know. It was just an obstacle away as he carried Chip out, slung over his shoulder, back aching the whole way back to the *Mobius*.

The cargo bay doors closed, sealing the crew inside the belly of the *Mobius*. The dull grey of the painted steel walls was bathed in a flashing red strobe of the warning lights. Until the air pressure returned, the klaxon blared in silence. The cargo hold had no windows, and now that they were closed in, there was no way to view the destruction of the derelict ship that had so recently been their workplace.

"Nice to have real gravity again, eh, boss?" Roddy's voice crackled through the comm, despite him being within arm's reach. At just a bit over a meter tall, with prehensile feet and elongated arms, the laaku was a closer descendant of his chimp-like forbearers than Carl was of his hominid ancestors.

Carl just grunted in reply. Gravity was always nicer on the *Mobius*. It was a perk of keeping a proper merlin aboard and not some puffed up star-drive repairman. Didn't mean he needed to hear about it every time they came aboard. He always liked that there was no weather to talk about in space. It made spacers a bit more interesting than planetside folk—until some four-handed mechanic decided to start yammering about the gravity.

Mriy cuffed Roddy upside the helmet, sending him stumbling—not that Roddy ever fell, with four limbs so close to the ground. She slouched against the wall, waiting out the pressurization cycle with her usual ill temper. It was her usual posture, leaving her eye to eye with her captain. Drawn up to full height, standing tall on her backward-bending legs and throwing her shoulders back, she could tower over any of the crew.

"You're at eighty percent," Tanny called over the comm from the door. She caught Carl's eye and gave a tight smile that was probably meant to be supportive, but just looked sickly. Tanny looked like a wreck. Against the pale contrast of her spacer's skin, it was easy to make out the telltale redness in her eyes.

Along with the air rushing back in to fill the cargo hold came the klaxon's repetitive honking. It kept up its monotonous, headache-inducing chant until air pressure was back to standard. The red lights stopped spinning, and an eerie quiet was left in the hold.

Mriy was the first to tear off her helmet. She shook loose her fur and smoothed it back with a gloved hand. She was azrin, and appeared to be a humanoid house cat with a shock of longer fur on the scalp reminiscent of a lion's mane. She was white, with splashes of orange, an unusual coloration among her kind. Chip had looked it up on the omni once and told her that made her a harlequin orange—he got a claw scar for his troubles, and they never spoke of it again.

Carl gave his helmet a weary twist and broke the seal, letting his ears pop and allowing the stale, familiar smell of hydraulic fluid and recycling purifiers in before taking it off completely. He sighed as he let go of the minty freshness that the scent infuser line added to his suit. Best thirty terra he ever spent. He no longer had to smell his own sweat and breath for hours on end every time he wore it.

Roddy was the last to start removing his suit, helmet and gloves, but the first to finish, thanks to having quadridexterous hands and feet working in concert. Laaku, Roddy's people, were closest species that humans had found to themselves, descended from chimp-like primates instead of the great apes. He ambled over toward where the escape pod sat with the window facing them. There had been no sign of the two occupants while the hold re-pressurized. "We should see about our passengers."

The door to the rest of the ship opened. Tanny came through with her head down, making straight for Carl. He braced himself, knowing it was coming, but she still squeezed the breath from his lungs when she wrapped her arms around him. Carl had a few centimeters on her, and a couple dozen kilos, but Tanny had arms like the marine she used to be. He held his helmet away and pulled her head against his shoulder with his free hand. She sobbed.

"It's my fault," Carl whispered to her. "Never should have let the kid work on that pod. Roddy could've done it right, with no one hurt."

Tanny's head twisted back and forth under his hand. "He was always ... too sure ... thought he knew it all."

The door burst open again and a gawky middle aged man strode in. His hair was black, except for a few insidious grey hairs that lurked here and there. His face wrinkled around a congenial grin and a pair of hazel eyes that focused like lasers wherever he aimed them—not that he was the sort who would have any luck with lasers. He wore battered old denim pants and a loose, hooded pullover, both stained with splotches of condiments and meaty juices, spit-scrubbed with a cloth and still deemed "more or less clean."

"What have we got?" Mort asked, slapping his hands together and rubbing them like he was trying to start a fire.

Carl shot Mort a glare as Tanny continued to sob more quietly against him. Mort stopped in his tracks and ducked, grimacing as he nodded and met Carl's eyes. "*Oops. Sorry,*" he mouthed. He cleared his throat. "Real shame. The Dyson boy wasn't half bad, as techsters go. Still, when you wrangle daily with technological forces beyond your understanding, it's a risk you have to accept. He'll be missed."

A clunk and a hiss of released sealant gas echoed across the hold. Roddy had convinced the escape pod that it had finished escaping and could let its charges free. Carl patted Tanny on the back. "I've gotta go. Captain stuff. Can't let them go thinking Roddy's in charge here, or they'll climb right back in."

As Carl walked across the hold, Mort took over the task of comforting Tanny. "Oh, you should have stuck around to watch. Tumbling across the cosmos like Lucifer's own bowling league.

Smashed that little pile of gizmos and contraptions to confetti. Reminds you just how little tech can really do, once you pit it against the powers of creation."

Carl shook his head and checked to see who was stepping out of the pod. First out was the boy, older than he had guessed. Chip had called him a boy, but Carl might have credited him with ten or twelve years, more a lad than a boy by that age, for all the good semantics did. He was skinny, which meant he either ate little, ran around a lot, or was just that sort of skinny, wimpy kid that gets picked on wherever they pop up. Carl knew that type well. The lad had mop-cut blond hair, tousled and streaked with bits of a darker shade. His eyes were a mystery, since he kept them aimed firmly at his feet. The clothes on his back were all midnight blue, cut in the style of some sort of school uniform.

Following him out was a young woman dressed in a black, shapeless robe that covered her from hair to ankles, leaving only the oval of her face and her hand uncovered. That face was alabaster white and straight from an artist's sketch. Smooth. That was the word for it. High cheekbones, thin nose, and the rest pulled close and smoothed like clay. If it were not for the vivid blue of her eyes, she would not have looked much different on a monochrome display. The only decoration she wore was a pendant shaped like a lowercase T.

"We're no threat to you," were the woman's first words. She looked straight at Carl while she said them. "Please, don't harm the boy."

"Dunno who said anything about harming," Carl replied. "We just saved your asses from an asteroid. A few minutes more on that wreck, and you'd have been dusted."

"Far be it from me to question altruism, but I think the ship might have gotten out of the way fine on its own if you hadn't blasted it full of holes."

Carl watched her face as she spoke, listened to inflections. He heard the words and they registered somewhere, but he did not expect to get much out of them. Her accent sounded Martian, one of the snootier cities at that, drawing out the end of the last word in every sentence. Carl would take a girl with an accent from any of the old Earth languages over a silver spoon Martian.

"You got us wrong, lady," said Carl. "We got your distress call, found a pirate picking over a fresh kill, drove him off. Wasn't us shot your ride full of hot plasma."

"All plasma's hot," Roddy muttered out the side of his mouth from Carl's elbow.

"Anyway, we could have left you there to die, and we didn't," Carl said. "That's gotta put in a good word for us. Lost us a man in the doing, too." Carl hung his head.

The fear in the woman's face softened. "Peace to you and yours. May I be of aid in your time of grief?"

Carl grimaced, realizing he should have recognized the pendant. "You a priestess?"

"I'm Sister Theresa Richelieu, of the One Church."

Tanny had composed herself, and she and Mort came over to join the welcome party. "Thought the One Church wasn't the Seeker type; uppity-ups not too big on travel," said Mort. "If the past won't come back, beat the future with a stick until it cries 'uncle?'"

"Some branches are like that," Sister Theresa agreed.

"How's it a One Church if it has branches?" Tanny asked.

Carl whistled, a quick burst with his fingers between his lips to draw everyone's attention. "You can get into theology on your own time. We got us a few tasks left before we can kick up our feet. Let's get the introductions out of the way.

"This is Tanny, our pilot. Roddy's our mechanic. Mriy ... well, what Mriy does around here's not important right now. Mort's our ship's wizard. If you have any a-tech with you, I'd set it aside before getting too close to him. And I'm Carl, Carl Ramsey,

Captain of the *Mobius*." He pulled off the EV suit glove from his right hand and held it out. Sister Theresa looked down at it a moment as if trying to decide whether to take it. When she finally shook Carl's hand, she had the grip of a child and skin as soft as peach skin.

An hour later, everyone had changed into their daily clothes, the cargo hold had been tidied, but far from inventoried, and they had reconvened in the hold.

"Thank you for doing this," Tanny whispered to Sister Theresa. They stood in a circle around Chip's body, still in his EV suit. As a small grace, they had left his face obscured by the darkened glass of the helmet.

Sister Theresa spoke at length about life and death, using ancient, dusty allegories and solemn assurances of the life beyond. Much of it was spoken in Latin, and Carl was tempted to pluck the earring from his ear so it would stay that way. The enchantment Mort had put on it turned everything into Earth Standard English—though it left Martian accents alone. Latin was one of those tongues that was clunky in translation, like Temerling or Straaka. It was meant to have a sound to it, like something you would recite to conjure demons, or to send them away. Instead, it sounded like a xeno trying to act tough in broken English.

Carl found himself fixated on the clumsiness of the words and not the message. He was unprepared when it ended.

"...Amen. Would any of you like to say a few words?"

Tanny nodded and took a half step forward. She looked at the helmet as she spoke. "Chip, I'm sorry. I'm not sure how I'll tell Aunt Sara and Uncle Bart, but I'll let them know you died saving two people's lives." She stepped back into the circle.

Everyone looked to everyone else. Sister Theresa caught Carl's eye and raised an eyebrow at him. Carl swallowed, knowing he really ought to say something as well.

"Charles Bartholomew Dyson, known as Chip because you thought it made you sound like you knew computers. Well, name or no name, you did. I was your captain. I was supposed to watch over you. Dammit, I should have made Roddy give you lessons in using a plasma torch." That was not the tone he was looking for. He needed something more profound. "Um, we are all dust in the wind, just drops of water in an endless stream. There is nothing to fear but fear itself. Don't fear the reaper. Um, Amen."

He glanced sidelong at the priestess, and Sister Theresa gave him a tight little smile and a nod.

"And now, in the tradition dating back to the sailing ships of Earth, we commend this body to the deep," said Carl. He leaned toward Tanny and muttered. "We on course?" She nodded.

With that, Mort muttered beneath his breath and lifted a hand; Chip's body rose from the floor. The old wizard led a short procession to the airlock and they shut the body inside. A moment later Chip was on course for the sun at the center of the Seles System.

"Tanny, get us a new course before we follow him in. Mriy, take our guests to their temporary quarters." Carl added under his breath: "We've got a free bunk."

Carl trudged up the steps, boots ringing on the steel mesh treads, heading for the common area. When he arrived, Mort was already there, slumped on the couch in front of a holovid—a detective story set in the early 2200s by the costumes. Carl grunted a greeting as he passed by on his way to the kitchen. Digging in the cupboards, he found a ham rod and a cheese rod, and fed them into the processor. After a quick check of the bread and mustard levels, he keyed in his order.

"What're you watching?" Carl asked as his lunch was being prepared. He shivered. The chill in the *Mobius* was always refreshing after sweating his ass off in the EV suit. With his sweat cooled, it was time to find something warmer than a thin kevlex shirt. A battered leather jacket hung on the wall, and Carl slung it on as he waited.

"Some claptrap Tanny's been nagging me to watch," said Mort. "It's all drivel. I had the murderer figured out from the first scene. Not like yelling it to them will get it solved any faster, either."

"I think they usually do that on purpose. You're supposed to watch how they figure it out."

"Bah, load of ass-backward mind candy. All sweet, no savor. Be a lad and find me something worth watching." Mort tossed Carl the remote. Carl slipped it into a jacket pocket without giving it more than a glance.

"Sure thing." The food processor dinged, and he grabbed the ham sandwich that came out, along with a beer from the fridge. "Just wanna talk to you about something first."

Mort patted Carl on the arm as the captain sat down beside him. "Good enough words. No one's expecting a captain to be Marcus Antonius. Metaphor's a clumsy tool in the hands of a—"

"No, not that. Our guests."

Mort's face twisted in a sneer. "I'd steer clear of that one. There's a sniff of foul science on her. Those aren't the looks she was born to have."

"Figured as much. Some sort of knife-work."

"More knife than fork to her, that's for sure," said Mort. "Odd for a pious girl to be so vain, wouldn't you say? Ought to have spent more time on her Latin, less on keeping her looks. Dreadful pronunciation. Keeps a charm, too, just so you know."

"It's a holy cross. Don't see many of those outside Sol."

"Carl, I'm not a blithering idiot. I grew up in Boston, remember? I've seen a crucifix or two before. She's got something else, hidden beneath those robes. Might just be more cosmetics. Got hit bad with an ugly-stick, decided to come after it from both ends, science and magic. Then again, maybe it's a death charm, ready to end her life if she gets captured. I'll know piss-all until I can get a closer look."

Carl nodded. "I'll keep my guard up. What about the boy?"

"What about him?"

Carl held up an open beer and a sandwich as he shrugged. "You tell me."

"Boy's a boy. Get back to me in ten years, and I might have an opinion of him. He's just had a nasty scare on one starship, now he's on another. Might be technology's scarred him for life." Mort turned aside and furrowed his brow. "Hmm, might be that we can make a wizard of him," he murmured to himself.

"I'd settle for him being a computer prodigy. But we're not that kind of lucky."

Carl pulled out the remote and flipped through the ship's library as he ate. They were out of range of the omni, and it wasn't worth firing up an astral link to connect from the middle of nowhere. Most of the files were Chip's or Tanny's, but the rest of them had a few favorites logged as well. He found one that might keep Mort amused for a while.

"Here you go. Zero-G cage fighting. You can thank Mriy."

Sandwich comfortably digesting in his stomach, Carl climbed down the steps to Chip's old quarters, keeping hold of both handrails. At the bottom he reached for the door handle but caught himself. He knocked.

"You may enter," said Sister Theresa, muffled by hull-rated steel.

Carl let himself in. The quarters were mostly how Chip had left them, with the soiled laundry moved from the bed to a neat pile on the floor. It was stacked with electronics and outfitted with more communications gear and computing power than the *Mobius's* main systems. "Getting settled?"

Sister Theresa gave him a wan smile. "We'll manage. When the world stops spinning around me, I'll help arrange Charles's things. I'm sure his family will want them."

"Tanny is family. And no one called him Charles. Speaking of, what's the boy called?"

"His name is Adam."

"He yours?"

For the first time, Sister Theresa showed some color on those pale cheeks. She flushed a pale pink. "Heavens, no! My vows forbid me from—"

"Yeah, sorry. Skip it. You look a little young for one that age, though I've seen stranger things," said Carl. To the boy, he said, "Hey, Adam, head on up those steps, go find yourself a bite. Just help yourself. I gotta have a talk with your friend here."

Adam nodded and slipped out the door. Before he got three steps, Carl called after him. "Hey Adam, you any good with computers?"

The boy turned and looked down the steps. He seemed a normal young boy for the first time since he left the escape pod. "I'm the best. I can beat anyone at Neptune Squad, Death Arena, and Omnithrust Racer."

Carl nodded. "Great kid. Good for you." He slammed the door shut.

Sister Theresa looked at Carl with wide eyes and clutched her crucifix tight in her fist. She swallowed. "So, this is the price of passage?"

"Whuh?" Carl furrowed his brow. "No! Hell no!" He waved his hands in front of him and backed himself against the closed door. "Nothing like that. Shit, and sorry about my language. No, we've just got a few things to discuss, seeing as you're with us until our next stop."

"What sort of things? I promise you; we won't leave these quarters."

Carl wiped a hand over his face. "What'd Mriy tell you? Never mind, just forget her. You aren't prisoners. Just stay out of the engine room, the cockpit, and the cargo hold. Rest of the ship, feel free. Just mind that you don't go into someone else's quarters, they're liable to get the wrong idea about you."

"Thank you," Sister Theresa smiled. "So was that all?"

"Hell, no. That wasn't even the preamble. I want to know what you were doing with the boy. You had hours to come up with a story, maybe even had something cooking for days before that. I expect it to be a good one. After that, you're going to tell me the truth."

"Captain Ramsey, it's really very simple—"

"Carl. Port authorities call me Captain Ramsey. And I'm damned sure this isn't simple. Priestesses aren't known for traveling much, and I should know because I'll take just about any kind of passengers I can get. You lot swear off children, and you don't make house calls to go picking up orphans. I'll let you continue, but just bear in mind."

The priestess's eyes searched the room for escape. The quarters aboard the *Mobius* doubled as the ship's escape pods—palatial by pod standards, small for bedrooms. To one side was an arrangement of glassteel panels forming a window looking into the Black Ocean—the last frontier of mankind, infinitely vast. To the other side was a closed door with Carl leaning against it, blocking the only exit.

"Let me make this easy on you," said Carl when she didn't

respond. "Everyone here's got secrets. That's why they aren't someplace better than this old bucket. I got 'em, too. I keep 'em safe. I keep 'em *all* safe. Everyone's. How can I do that? I gotta know what I'm protecting. I can't be having shit rain down around me over stuff I can't see coming. Too many lives are at stake. You level with me; I don't judge. Play it straight up and the worst thing I'll do is feed the both of you, loan you a bunk, and drop you off at the next stop. Understand me?"

Sister Theresa nodded.

"Then let's start with something basic. You kidnap that boy?"

The priestess looked away. "No."

"That's strike one," said Carl. He took a finger and aimed her chin back in his direction. "You slip up twice more, and you spend the rest of the trip in the escape pod we found you in, and that's how we deliver you to the law. So you have a good reason taking the boy?"

"Yes." She nodded.

Carl let out a sigh. "Good. You're a shitty liar, so this is going to go easy if you just keep sticking to the truth. So you had a good reason...what was it?"

Sister Theresa sat there a moment, chewing at the inside of her cheek.

Carl came and sat down beside her on the bed. "I'm counting that as your second strike. Let me put this into terms you maybe understand a bit better. This here, this is my ship. It's like my church, and you're in it. It's time for you to confess your sins, but instead of repenting them, we're going to make them right; we're going to find a way to live with them.

"Or you can go right in the escape pod," said Carl. "Your call, but confession is good for the soul. Start at the beginning: are you even really a priestess?"

"Not officially, not anymore," Sister Theresa said. "I'm sure they've defrocked me by now, and I was only probationary to begin with. Before that I taught fourth grade at the school on Bentus VIII, at a church school. Adam was one of my students."

"I'm with you so far. What made you run off with him?"

"It's a small planet, mostly corporate. There's not a lot going on that Harmony Bay Corporation doesn't own. It was a research facility for them. In my class, there were a dozen like him...Adam, Benjamin, Caleb, David, Elijah, Felix..."

"They're cloning?"

Sister Theresa nodded. "Not just cloning, they're trying to rewrite the boys' minds, make them into customized people, data storage couriers, what have you. It's not just one plan; it's experimentation to see what they can do."

Carl ran a hand over his scalp, digging his fingers through hair that was five hours in an EV suit past needing a shower. "I get it now. You managed to rescue one of them."

"Not just one of them—Adam, the original. He's the one they cloned from. They're all in school together so they can judge the clones against him, see what they do better and worse. The scientists' children attend as well, but more than half my class were Adam's clones."

Carl nodded along, trying the pieces and seeing where they did not fit. "And how did you know what they were doing? Picking up on the clones, sure, I buy that. What about those plans for them? Doesn't seem like the type of stuff they'd tell the local schoolteacher."

"Are you a God-fearing man, Captain Carl?"

Carl leaned away, straightening from his seated position. That question caught him off guard, but fair was fair. He was asking a lot about her. "Me? Naw. If God was still the smiting type, I think I'd have gotten dusted years ago, back in my Navy days. He had plenty of chances after that, too. I'm a believer, don't get me wrong, but I've got plenty of time to settle up with Him before I'm done. I'm sure picking up one of his young minions on a mission of mercy won't look too shabby for me, either."

"Well, not every man of science is deaf to God's word. Dr. James Augustus Cliffton was one of the top scientists for Harmony Bay. He was an old man, and worried about his standing in the eyes of the Lord. He wanted to make amends for what he helped create. He helped us: access codes, transport schedules, a little money. Without his help, I'd still be wondering what was going on with all the identical boys in my class."

"What're you planning to do with him? Raise him as your own?"

"I ... I hadn't thought that far ahead. Just getting away seemed like such a ... such a ..."

"Herculean task?" Carl suggested. She nodded.

"I have to ask, now that I've told you," said Sister Theresa. "That ship you said you drove off, could it have belonged to Harmony Bay?"

Carl waved off her concern. "Naw. That heap wasn't corporate. Bigger question, would they call in a kidnapping, or would they handle it themselves?"

"I ... I couldn't say."

"Well, either way, we can't be having a defrocked priestess going around in a getup like that. Head down to the cargo hold and find yourself something inconspicuous in the luggage we salvaged. If you find your own stuff, great. If not, just pick something that fits. You got a name from before you joined the church?"

"Esper. My parents named me Esper Theresa. And I thought you said I couldn't go to the cargo bay."

"That was before I knew you."

Carl headed down before Esper got herself settled in enough to want a change of clothes. The interior of the *Mobius* looked like someone had set off an explosive charge in an open-air bazaar. Footlockers lay in poorly stacked heaps, while their contents were strewn across the floor in rough piles by type. One of the footlockers had been repurposed to collect currency found among the luggage. P-tech was jumbled into a rough pile while A-tech was laid out neatly to keep it from getting damaged. Sentimental items were clustered near the bay door, unsettling reminders that everything had once belonged to living people with families and friends of their own. Clothing had the largest share of the space— a two-meter high mountain of cloth made from every sort of plant, animal, and chemical known in ARGO space. Roddy and Mriy were hard at work cutting open the remaining footlockers.

"First impressions?" Carl called out as he crossed the hold. He fished a pair of dark glasses from his jacket pocket to protect against the flare of the plasma torches.

Roddy cut through a lock and flicked his torch off. "They seem harmless enough. Might be nice having a blessing on the ship." He threw back his head and downed the rest of the beer in his hand, tossing the empty can into the pile with the personal items.

"If we end up killing the woman," Mriy said, "may I keep the little one as a pet? I can make up a bed for him in my quarters."

"I meant the loot," Carl replied. "Anything worth keeping?"

"Take your pick of the boutique," Roddy said, jerking the thumb of one foot at the pile of garments. "Everything looks human in there. Nothing my size."

"Mort been down yet?"

"He took one look and said to let him know when we were done," said Roddy. "If you're looking for him, he's probably filling his burger-hole in the lounge, gaping at the holovid."

Mriy shut off her plasma torch. "Carl, come look!" Her pupils were wide behind her welding goggles, nearly circular, her fangs bared in a grin. Roddy beat Carl to Mriy's side, curiosity lending speed to his low-slung body. "This symbol is like the Earth woman's pendant."

Mriy pointed to a book lying atop a pile of folded clothes in the footlocker she had just cut open. Carl was tempted to protest that Esper was Martian, but he was more interested in seeing what her belongings contained. The book's title was *The Holy Bible*, which went along well with the Sister Theresa story. Carl pushed past Mriy and rummaged through the rest. A children's datapad, well scuffed from use. Several articles of women's clothing, all drab and conservative, even the undergarments. A silver box with a few pieces of costume jewelry. Two school uniforms. A tiny case containing toiletries.

"Airlock," Carl said.

"But wait, this is all her stuff, isn't it?" Roddy asked.

"She's on the run with that boy of hers. She's Esper, he's Adam, and there was never a priestess on board. If anyone asks, the boy is her half brother; I'll work out some details if he needs a better cover later."

Mriy pointed to the bible. "Bad business defiling a holy book. I want no part."

Carl pursed his lips and stared down at the book, lying atop the sloppily repacked belongings. The fake gold lettering stared up at him accusingly. The synthetic leather cover was worn from handling; someone had loved that book. He held it up and riffled through to see if anything fell out. The dingy grey paper held no secrets trapped between pages.

It was temping to throw all the problems away at a go. Carl's hand twitched toward the footlocker, to throw it back. "Here, take it back to your quarters if you don't want the bad mojo." He pressed the book into Mriy's hands. "I sent Esper to shower before coming to pick out new clothes from the heap here. You've got 'til she gets out to hide it. Roddy, I'll give you a hand venting this thing to vacuum."

He pointed to each of them, his best captain's glare in his eyes. "Not a word of this. She already mourned this junk once already. No point getting her hopes up, just to smash them. It's gotta go."

"What do I do with this?" Mriy asked, turning the book over in her hands. "I barely read ape."

"Stow it or give it to Mort when Esper's not around. Mort loves books."

***

The cockpit always had the best view, even when there was no view to be had. The Black Ocean went out to infinity, but the eye made you think that the stars were right there just out of arm's reach. Between star systems there was nothing. Lots and lots of nothing. There was more nothing than all the something in the galaxy combined. And it was beautiful. Peaceful.

The inside of the cockpit, however, was anything but. A faint rush from the air circulator never let it get completely silent. Indicator lights demanded attention, even when they had nothing important to show. The navigation display showed an icon representing the *Mobius* surrounded on all sides by void, even with the scale set to maximum; a line still spun around though, constantly updating the lack of anything to see. Jazz poured softly from the speakers. Tanny slouched in the pilot's chair, her feet up on the console, a datapad in hand.

Carl crept up under cover of a Miles Davis piece he could not put a name to. He peered over the pilot's seat and read the datapad Tanny held. He took one more quiet step to the side and threw himself into the copilot's chair, slumping with his legs over the arm. "A hundred men you should never date?" he asked, quoting the article title from the datapad. "How many times am I in there?"

"You keep those hands of yours off the controls or I'll break your wrists," Tanny replied, eyes wide and brow low. Carl held up his hands in the classic bank robbery victim pose. "What do you want?"

"I'm still sorry about Chip."

That took the edge off Tanny. She settled back into her seat and flicked the datapad off. "I'll write something to his folks tomorrow. Not like they have any reason to be expecting anything."

"I can have Mriy come up and watch the void for you, if you'd rather take the night off."

"Someone's gotta cover Chip's shift," said Tanny. "Might as well be me."

"I wanted to talk to you about the priestess we picked up."

"Oh yeah, the prom queen of Uncanny Valley."

"I'm trying to ignore that, but she does sort of have a weird look to her. Almost familiar."

"Did your sisters ever collect dolls?" Tanny asked.

"Holy shit!" said Carl. He slapped a hand gently against his forehead. "Susie Sunshine. Yeah, Jamie collected those. She's a dead ringer."

"Actually it was the Vicky Valentine doll I was thinking of. Same collection though. I used to collect those."

"So what, we've got a doll fanatic aboard?"

Tanny's expression soured. "Nah, those were a while back. I was on the young side to still be playing with those, and I bet I've got eight or ten years on that priestess." Tanny had never been shy about her age—or anything much, really. Carl always liked that about her. "It's probably her mother."

Carl's nose wrinkled as his brow scrunched. "That's sick.

How many times you think she had to go under, to look like that?"

Pieces. That was why Carl liked talking to people. No one figured out a whole puzzle on his own, at least not someone like Carl. Different people picked up on different things. It helped being able to tell who was full of shit and who was telling it straight, but talk to enough people and you can get to the bottom of almost anything.

Tanny shrugged. "I'm no vanity surgeon. A dozen, twenty, a hundred? More than she could stomach is a good bet."

"Shitty childhood, runs off to join the church?" Carl asked. Tanny nodded. "Might explain why she took the boy."

"They're not related, are they?"

"Nope, just one lost soul rescuing another."

A torrent of water washed over Carl's bare skin. It was tepid, just warm enough not to make him shiver. Still, it felt good to wash away the grime from helping Roddy in the cargo bay. He opened his mouth and gargled the water that filled it. There was a metallic aftertaste when he spat it into the shower drain—the reprocessor was just one more thing for Roddy to fix.

From outside the shower, Carl heard the muffled sound of the ship-wide comm. He reached for the controls and shut off the shower flow. "Carl? CARL? Get your ass up here, pronto!" Tanny shouted over the speakers.

Carl hustled through the ship with a towel around his waist, his hair dripping and his bare feet slapping against the steel deck plates.

"Go find out what's she blathering about," Mort said from his seat on the couch in the common room. Mriy glanced up from the game of Death Arena she was playing against Adam, and the boy did not even flinch from the holovid screen.

Esper poked her head up from the stairwell to Chip's old quarters. "What's going on?" Her cheeks were flushed, and she was short of breath.

Carl did not stop to answer, but continued along the short corridor and up to the cockpit, one hand holding his towel closed.

"What's wrong?" he asked Tanny when he opened the cockpit door.

"Look." She pointed to the console.

It was a text-only communique: UNIDENTIFIED VESSEL, POWER DOWN AND PREPARE TO BE BOARDED. ARGO AUTHORITY: (ENV) TALLY-HO.

"What should I say?" she asked after a pause to let Carl process the message. She leaned away from him. "And stop dripping on me."

"Full stop. Transmit our coordinates," Carl replied. "Not like we've got anything to hide. Rather let them rummage around than risk finding they've started outfitting customs ships with top-line engines."

"You *sure* we're clean?" Tanny asked. "Like, Navy inspection clean?"

Carl furrowed his brow and ran his fingers through his dripping hair. "Mort's got our unmentionables sealed up tight. We've got legit salvage in the hold ..."

"She means me," said Esper from the corridor just outside the cockpit. She had changed into clothes from the salvage pile in the cargo hold. Baggy black pants brushed the floor, held in place by a wide belt. A sleeveless pink blouse covered her to the neck but left her midriff exposed. At a glance, Carl could not tell if she wore her pendant beneath it, but she looked nothing like a priestess.

"You hotter than you let on?" Carl asked. "What happened to that story about a rescue?"

"The boy's not mine. Even if Harmony Bay didn't report Adam kidnapped, we can't explain why *we* have him. He's got parents on Mars."

"Your call," Tanny said, her hands hovering over the controls.

Carl looked Esper in the eye. She was scared; that much was plain. But what did it mean? Was she concerned for her own skin, the boy, or something else she failed to mention? "Send it," he said, nodding to Tanny. "Wait. On second thought, open a comm."

"Might take a minute. Who knows how far they are behind us? They're not even in sensor range."

Carl ran a hand over the stubble on his face, options whirring in his head. He nodded absently. "You," he said, pointing to Esper, "are the only survivor of that wreck. We pulled you out during the salvage after your escape pod jammed, except you were the only one in it. Got that?"

"I think so."

"I want you to *believe* that's what happened. I'll try to keep them from asking you too many questions; you just had a major shock after all. But if they do, you've gotta keep them off Adam's trail. Now go back and tell Mort to stash Adam in his quarters. Clean out Chip's bunk and take anything Adam touched and send it with Mort, too. Go."

Esper nodded and hurried back down the corridor.

Tanny closed her eyes and shook her head. "You never change."

"The easy way's never the best one. Once you start running from every little thing, you can't ever stop."

The console beeped. Tanny keyed the comm. "Unidentified ship, this is Earth Navy Vessel Tally-ho. Coordinates received. Hold position and prepare for customs inspection per ARGO transportation code 97312.3.1." The voice was smooth and professional, as bland an Earth accent as you could get, shy of a computer.

Carl smiled. There was something familiar about that voice. He reached for the button to open the mic. Tanny slapped his hand away. He reached around her on the other side, and she slapped his hand again. "Stop that."

"Get out of my cockpit and dry off."

"Just ... key it for me, then. Would you?"

Tanny pursed her lips, but held down the button as requested. "*Tally-ho*, this is *Mobius*. Your signal checks out. Can't be too careful this far out in the Black Ocean. You won't get any trouble out of us. Thanks for keeping the borderlands safe. *Mobius* out." He nodded to Tanny and she closed the comm.

"What?"

"What what?"

"That grin."

"I thought you liked surprises," said Carl. He slicked back his dripping hair and flicked droplets of water in Tanny's direction as he left the cockpit.

"I hate surprises," she called after him. "You *know* that."

Carl came up the steps from his quarters two at a time, bending in half at the waist to keep from hitting his head on the ceiling of the narrow stairwell. He was dried and dressed, wearing denims and his battered leather jacket. Once he reached the common room, he had the overhead clearance to pull on an equally battered old Earth Navy dress cap. He stopped and blinked to take in the scene before him.

"The hell's all this?" he asked. Esper sat at the edge of one of the dinner table chairs, back straight and hands clasped as if they were keeping each other from running away screaming. Mriy was lying spread full length on the couch, asleep to all appearances, her bare feet twitching. On the kitchen counter, Roddy was four-fisting cans of Earth's Preferred. The tables in the kitchen and rec areas of the common room were both arrayed with the personal weapons the crew kept on board, from blades to blasters—it was the only thing Carl could see that was right about the picture.

"What?" Esper asked, jerking her head around at the sound of his voice.

"I asked you all to be ready when they got here," said Carl, spreading his arms.

Roddy belched. "You expect me to be civil while I'm sober?"

"Relaxed. Amiable. Helpful. What I see is scared shitless, sleeping, and half-drunk." He grabbed two of the beers away from Roddy. He plunked one of them down on the table by Esper, between a stun rifle and one of Mriy's bone dueling knives. "Drink up."

"But I don't—"

"Can it," said Carl. "And I mean *can* it. You can't be tight as an E-string when the inspection crew gets here."

He took the second beer over to Mriy and held the can as if to pour it over her face as she lay snoring softly. There was no flinch; she really was asleep. Much as he hated *ever* waking her, he took a swig of the beer himself and kicked the couch. Mriy stirred and opened one eye in a squint.

"They here yet?" Mriy asked. She yawned, revealing a mouth full of fangs the size of Carl's fingers—and stinking of rotted *taru*.

"Tanny's feeding them candy glass down in the hold," Roddy replied. He took a chug of his beer. "They're Navy though, so there's only so long she's gonna be able to put up a smiley for them."

"We had candy left?" Carl asked.

"Hell, no," Roddy replied. "Figurative ... you know."

Hearing footsteps coming up from below, Carl threw himself against the nearest wall, feigning a casual slouch. He pulled his navy cap low and crossed his arms. A grin worked itself onto his face, but he fought it back and relaxed his facial muscles before the footsteps reached the common room.

"Which one of you is captain of this ship?" The navy officer who spoke was soft and doughy, with a crisp navy blue uniform making his build appear solid rather than sloppy. He carried a datapad and wore a blaster sidearm at his hip. He scanned the room with professional annoyance.

"Hey, Dingo? What're you up to out past nowhere? They punish you for something?" Carl asked.

The navy officer's eyes narrowed. "Who the hell are—?" Carl pushed up the brim of his cap and smiled. "Blackjack, you bastard! How've you been? Wait, don't answer that; must be shitty if you're flying this heap of castoff parts."

"Hey, don't talk about my crew like that," Carl replied with indignation. He addressed the crew scattered around the room, including Tanny, who lingered in the doorway. "This is an old buddy of mine, Ted Wellington. He used to be a half decent fighter pilot before he put on twenty kilos and those scrambled eggs on his collar."

"Hey, I outrank *you* now, hotshot," Wellington replied.

"I promoted myself to captain when I bought *Mobius*," Carl replied.

Wellington snorted. "You retired as a Lieutenant Commander though, and that's what really counts. You can call yourself emperor of this tub for all I care."

"Retired?" Carl scoffed. "Do I *look* retired to you? You were in the hold. I was on that transport, hauling salvage right along with the rest of my crew."

"About that ... I'm going to need records of that salvage op.

Your first officer told me ..." Wellington trailed off. He paused to look at Tanny. "I thought you looked familiar. Tanny?"

She smiled. "Hey, Dingo. I didn't recognize your voice over the comm, but Carl did, apparently."

"Carl?"

"My middle name. I stopped going by Brad when I mustered out. Keeps things compartmentalized. Anyone who calls me Brad's from back home. Don't hear Blackjack much these days."

"So what's Carl do with a hodgepodge old diplomatic shuttle with more scrapyard parts than original?"

Carl shrugged. "Little of this and that."

A pair of marines entered with blaster rifles at the ready, as if Carl and his crew were going to ambush them. Behind them, a small squadron of techs tromped in with scanning equipment.

"Hey, watch it with that stuff," Roddy said from the counter. He gestured with a beer can at the navy scanners.

"Ahh, yes," Wellington said, as if noticing the other crew members for the first time. "She mentioned you had a couple xenos aboard."

"Wait a minute, now. Roddy's a full citizen. Phabian Two is an ARGO member."

"I'll verify that, but *that* isn't," Wellington said, hooking a thumb at Mriy. Her eyes tracked him, but no other part of her moved. "You running a ship or a zoo?"

"C'mon Dingo, ease off," Carl said. "What're you boys doing tossing a little freighter like we were big bad pirates?"

Wellington raised an eyebrow. "I'm just hoping you're not smuggling anything. For an old pal, if you want to mention anything I might find that ... shall we say ... might not look good in an official report, I might be able to take care of it discreetly."

"I'm clean as your service record," Carl said with a grin. There was no objecting to that one with four of Wellington's own crew in the room. One of the techs cast him a surreptitious glance to check for a reaction. Wellington just frowned slightly.

"Have it your way."

"Just a 'so-you-know-it,' my ship's wizard is in the forward port cabin. I told him to stay there until you were done your inspection."

Wellington gave Carl a beleaguered glare. "You *know* I'm going to have to search his quarters. The old 'my wizard hates scanners' bit got old years ago."

"Mine's a little rough on A-tech," Carl replied. "You just might want to watch out for your shiny toys when you interview him."

"Another dreg in a crew of dregs?" Wellington glanced over at Tanny. "No offense. A grav-jockey who can't keep his magic in check for a simple scan?"

"Mort? Mort's not my star-drive mechanic. He's more like a partner—old family friend who comes along to see the sights. Keeping 'dark science' from invading his innards is a reflex. Just a warning, do whatever you want. I'm not the one who'll be stranded out in nowhere's back garden without a scanner and trying to explain it in a report."

"Fine. Give me his biographicals, and I can at least run a manual check in the system."

"His name's Mordecai The Brown, from Boston Prime, born—"

"Wait, I need his official name, not his professional title," said Wellington. Roddy snickered.

"That *is* his given name. Whole family's got "The" as a middle name; it's traditional. He's got a sister who married into the name Sarajah The McGowan."

The two techs exchanged a worried look.

Mort sat on the edge of his bed with his hands tucked into opposing sleeves of his sweatshirt. It was, all things considered, a dignified, wizardly pose. At his elbow sat a ten-year-old boy trying to mimic him, fingers trying to worm their way into sleeves too snug for them to fit. Mort elbowed Adam in the side to get him to stop fidgeting. One of the two techs scouring the room glanced over at Mort, but the wizard glared at her until she went back to her work.

"You know," the tech said to her colleague, "when the commander said we'd be checking a wizard's quarters, I expected more ..."

"More magic?" the other tech asked.

"Yeah," the female tech replied. "This stuff's all phony. The staff, the robes, it's like costume wizardry."

Adam looked at Mort with a question plain in his eyes. Mort put a finger to his lips and winked.

The techs opened the closet door, revealing Mort's drab wardrobe, as well as a hastily piled assortment of military-grade blaster power packs. They looked it over, each using their scanning equipment. Mort could only guess, but he assumed one was checking for magical objects, and the other for more mundane contraband.

"You sure you're a wizard?" the female tech asked. "Not just a street magician or something?"

Mort tapped his index fingers together, producing a spark. He graced the tech with a genial smile, but said nothing. She went back to her work, opening the cover to Mort's bookshelf and scanning the volumes. Mort squinted at the scanner, trying to make sense of the red blinking lights and flashing text that the tech was ignoring.

"Well, that'll do it," the male tech said.

"Yeah, I'm finished here, too," the female tech replied. "Sorry for the inconvenience."

When the door clanged shut behind them, Adam let out a long breath and slouched. "How did they not see me?"

Mort shrugged. "I don't know what those scientists left in that noggin of yours, but remember this: never fight a wizard on his own turf."

"The scanners *did* find stuff though."

Mort tapped a finger to his temple. "I de-attention-ified them. They could have been in a navy surplus yard or the grand chamber of the Convocation, they would have found the same thing: jack squat."

Esper sat frozen to her seat, staring at the back side of Commander Wellington's datapad. She could not look up into his eyes; couldn't even say what color they were. He held the scanning wand in front of her eye and a soft light shone briefly over her face.

"Miss Esper Theresa Richelieu," Wellington addressed her, butchering her last name and adding an extra syllable to it. "Says here you're from Mars. Where about?"

"New Singapore," she replied. The datapad must have said so. If that was the commander's idea of a test, maybe this wouldn't be so bad.

"There's no occupation listed. What is it you do for a living?"

"I'm currently between jobs," Esper replied.

"I understand you were the lone survivor of the *Regulon*," Wellington said. It was not a question, exactly, but he paused for a response.

Esper nodded. The back of the datapad was a light grey, the color of a pigeon's feathers, or a storm cloud. The hand that held it was thick-fingered, and one of those fingers bore a wedding band. It was simple in style, like the one Carl wore.

"Can you describe the events leading up to your ship's destruction?"

Esper swallowed. Wellington's cuff was starched stiff, and there was a comm built into it. It had false cufflinks with brass naval insignia. "I was just a passenger. First I knew of it was when the horns sounded that we were under attack. The ship shook a number of times, and there was an announcement to get to the escape pods. I got to mine late. I ... I had to launch it myself. I don't know if it was damaged or I did it wrong, but I got the pod stuck. Carl and his crew rescued me; a man named Chip died cutting me free." A fresh pang of guilt jabbed her in the stomach.

Esper's eyes strayed to Carl, sitting on the arm of the couch with the two armed marines looming over him. Immediately she focused on the back of the datapad once more. There was a scratch on the corner, perhaps two centimeters long. Parts of the back were worn smoother than the rest, near where Wellingon's fingers rubbed.

"And the identity of the attacking vessel?" Wellington asked. His tone hardened. This was what he really wanted. Esper relaxed, but tried not to show it, remaining stiff in her seat.

"I have no idea. Carl would know better than I," she replied. "I wasn't in any position to find out who attacked us."

"You're sure?" Wellington pressed. "No one rushing for the escape pods said anything? Mentioned a ship name? Described it?"

Esper shook her head. "No. Nothing."

"If you want, you can come aboard my ship. They can't hurt you, you're an ARGO citizen, and you're under my protection."

Esper's eyes darted to Carl for a fraction of a second, but Carl was gazing off into space, watching the stars through the glass panels in the common room roof. "I really have no idea."

Wellington tapped something on the datapad and it beeped.

"Very well. I've recorded that as your official statement. You can go if you like."

Esper nodded and headed for the stairwell to her borrowed quarters, treading the line between unseemly haste and lingering a single moment longer than she had to.

"You're an ass, Dingo," she heard Carl say just before shutting the door and buying herself enough privacy to sit down and cry.

Half an hour later, and with all the crew interviewed, the inspection and scanning crews reported in. Carl had lost count of them, but apparently there had been a dozen junior naval officers swarming through his little ship like bees in a hive. Wellington let Carl sit and listen to the officers' reports.

"... parts all have IDNs, none in the database as stolen ..."

"... this tub has a heavier shield generator than the *Tally-ho*. I don't think the engines even throw enough juice to fully power it ..."

"... guns check out. This thing is armed like an escort frigate, but all the readings are in the approved civilian range ... just *barely* ..."

"... no contraband, including the salvage. Looks like this lot wasted a lot of time cutting out the computer cores. No data anywhere. Must have been a hellacious EMP ..."

Carl swore under his breath. He had been counting on selling the cores with the data intact. Blanked and possibly EMP damaged, a transport's computers were worth only their spare-parts value.

"... no sign of stowaways, unreported crew or passengers, and no unauthorized plant or animal life. The two xenos have been IDed as Rodek of Kethlet, ARGO citizen from Phabian II, and an azrin from Meyang VII. We can't verify her claimed identity until we get signal from the core, but she says her name is Mriy Yrrsis ..."

Wellington nodded along with the reports as they came in, each officer departing for the airlock as he or she was dismissed. When they finished, just Wellington and his two marines remained with Carl, Tanny, Mriy, and Roddy in the common room.

"You people seem to be looking for trouble," Wellington observed, giving a nod to the pile of weapons spread on the table. He picked up a sword from the pile and drew it from its scabbard, revealing a black graphite blade with a graceful curve. "This isn't the sort of thing they taught in that fencing elective in flight school. You even know how to use one of these?"

"Not really," Carl replied. "But I'm a shit aim with a blaster, too, so what's the difference? It's sharp, won't ricochet off energy shields, and works around active magic." He shrugged. "I like to be prepared."

"Prepared ..." Wellington said. He slid the sword back into its scabbard. "Prepared like having engines running on three different fuel sources, guns that I'm lucky you're not aiming at my ship, a shield generator that you can't even get up to full power on a dinghy like this, and more obsidian-hardened systems than I've seen in a space-faring vessel."

"I heard obsidian keeps the gravity nice," Carl said sheepishly.

Wellington bounced on the balls of his feet. "Well, I'll say that much for you. This *is* nice gravity. You wouldn't believe how many times we get stuck combing through zero-g heaps. Crazy spacers who never set foot in a gravity well." He shook his head.

"You're welcome," said Tanny flatly. She sat with her arms crossed on the couch, willing Wellington off the ship. She had a special talent for making someone feel unwelcome. She had never gotten on with Wellington, even when they had first met.

"I've gotta ask, or it'll kill me wondering: what do you *do* with this thing?" Wellington asked. "I can't cite you for anything. You're a millimeter from breaking a dozen regulations, but you haven't. Why go to the trouble?"

Carl smirked. "I like feeling safe, but I want to see the sights in the galaxy. I don't want to be stuck where Earth Navy can protect me. Some folks pay good money to deliver things interesting places. I like good money."

"And yet you're cutting dead computer core from derelict transports?"

Carl raised his palms. "Work's been a little scarce."

"And what about your crew? No offense to any of you," Wellington added hastily. "But what the hell, Blackjack? You used to be an ace, now you're ... and these ... you let your ex-wife fly your ship for you?"

"They threatened to mutiny if I kept flying *Mobius*," Carl replied. "He may be mine, but the crew aren't. Tanny flew troop transports, and that's the sort of ride my crew prefers. They kept thinking they were going to die with me flying, so it was either let Tanny pilot, or watch everyone leave *Mobius*. Speaking of which ..."

Wellington nodded. "Yeah. So long, Captain Ramsey. Blackjack's a long way in your ion trail, huh?"

That evening, the crew and guests of the Mobius all gathered in the common room, under a ceiling that showed the stars above. The ship was on auto-pilot, limping out of ARGO controlled space. The *Tally-ho* had gone back to its own patrol route. The food fabricator was churning out dinner after dinner as everyone settled in to eat.

"I can't believe you did that for me," Esper said. "Thank you all so much."

"Mort did all the hard work," said Carl. "I nearly gave myself a hernia not laughing when those two wet-eared techs came out of your quarters like they'd just wasted their time."

"Think nothing of it," Mort replied. Roddy tossed a hamburger across the room, and it slowed to a drift as Mort collected it and reassembled the pieces that had drifted apart in flight. "I enjoy practicing the subtler arts once in a while. Their scanners were no match for my magic."

"You could have let me do all the hard work," Mriy said, slumping back on the couch with Adam tucked under her arm. She had eaten first and quickest, and was already finished. "We'd have two ships and plenty of money once we sold theirs."

"Last thing we need is ARGO hunting us down," said Tanny. "Don't we have enough enemies as it is?"

A quiet hung in the air as everyone carefully avoided delving into that particular subject. The only sounds were of eating and the ding of the food processor finishing meals.

"Guy was an asshole," Roddy said, breaking the silence. "Can't believe you were friends with that xenophobe."

"Friends?" Carl scoffed. "We called him Penny-Toad until he earned his wings. One of those spoiled navy brats who shows up to flight school with an admiral's last name. I made his life hell for a good two years."

"Should have done it my way," Mriy muttered, flexing a hand and extending her claws.

Carl winked at her. "I was tempted."

That night, Tanny sat alone in the cockpit, reading. There was no guessing the *Tally-ho's* sensor range, and they did not want to do anything but a slow drift until they were sure *Mobius* had some privacy. No matter their speed, the view outside the glassteel windows remained the same. There were times when she stopped to contemplate the dissonance of the ship. Outside, the majestic infinity, separated from them by a void so vast it defied imagination, with nothing but stray hydrogen atoms for light years. Inside, the sweat and stink of a half dozen sentients, the thrum of the engines through the ship, and the sound of Caro Jay and the Brainwaves trying to drown out Mriy and Mort's holovid blood sports.

A soft knock on the cockpit door startled her. Tanny juggled the datapad she was reading and pulled her feet off the co-pilot's armrest. "Who's there?" It was a stupid question, she knew. None of the crew knocked.

"It's me," Esper replied through the door. "Can I come in?"

Tanny opened the cockpit door. "Just don't touch anything."

Esper sat down gingerly in the co-pilot's seat and closed the door. "You know the captain well, right?"

Tanny opened her mouth to say something scathing. Something about Esper's earnestness gave her pause. "Not as well as you might think. But yeah, I guess I know Carl well enough."

"Please, if this is too personal, just tell me," said Esper. "I mean, you were married to him after all. But—"

"But what?"

"Can I trust him?"

Tanny burst out laughing. Esper paled, which was a trick considering how pale she started out. Tanny held up her hands to placate the priestess. "I'm sorry, but you just asked the trillionaire question there, didn't you?"

"He explained how to deceive that commander so simply. I ...

I can't imagine I got away with it. He must be a lot better himself."

She was a delicate creature, inside and out. Tanny had known girls like her; maybe not ones that looked so mannequin perfect, but ones that got by on looks and trust and luck. "Listen to me. You're a big girl now, and you can do whatever you want. But if you give that man your heart, he will put it in his back pocket and forget about it when he sits down. I can already see the little twinkles in your eye when you look at him. Snuff 'em out quick, or it'll hurt. I used to think I knew him better, that I could tell when he was being honest. Well, I've divorced him three times."

"Three times?" Esper asked, gaping at Tanny. "How the h— why would you do that?"

"The man can talk a pretzel straight, and be sweet enough to rot your teeth."

"Why do you still fly with him?"

"He's a good man and a good boss, just a shitty husband. Don't go breaking any vows over him; he's not worth it."

The stairs clanged beneath Carl's boots as he took them two at a time up to the common room. Mort sat on the couch with Adam, the two of them engrossed in a game of Omnithrust Racer. Carl hadn't even known they had a copy of it in the ship's computer, but right then he didn't care.

"We're good," said Carl, catching his breath. "Roddy's got everything back the way it belongs and Tanny just got me on the comm to say that the Tally-ho's been out of our sensor range for six hours—hopefully that puts us out of theirs."

Mort grunted.

Carl turned his attention to the racing game and saw that the two of them were neck and neck in the final straightaway of a course called "Tri-star Deathway," according to the in-game display. Mort rarely played active games, but was faring surprisingly well. With any luck he wouldn't get steamed and accidentally fry the controller if he lost.

"Yes!" Adam shouted, jumping from his seat. "That's five in a row!" The game played a victory theme as Adam's racer crossed the line in first place. Carl didn't know if he was better off congratulating the kid for winning or making fun of him for beating an old wizard who couldn't work a datapad.

Carl took the remote and shut off the display. "We're good for astral any time, Mort."

"Kid's lucky, that's all," he grumbled. He threw the controller across the room. Just before it smashed against the wall, it slowed to a drift and set itself gently into its recharger. "How deep you need us?"

"Nothing fancy," Carl replied. "Just someplace with a little zip, and none of the standard depths."

Mort disappeared into his room and returned with a gnarled staff of authentic, Earth-grown oak, older than everyone on board the *Mobius* put together. Carl had never thought to ask, but he had always assumed it pre-dated the ban on cutting trees in Earth's preserves. As Mort took up a position in the center of the common room, Carl keyed the comm panel by the door. "Keep out of the common room for a minute. Mort's taking us astral."

It was easy at times to think of Mort as just a grumpy old man who hated science. But watching him plant his staff in the center of the floor and begin his chant, it was hard to think of him as anything but a wizard. The words *felt* old, even though he had no idea what they meant. If God were the swearing type, Carl imagined that He would use some of those words in doing it. As the chant continued, symbols around the periphery of the common room floor began to glow a dull green.

"What are those?" Adam asked in a whisper, gaping at the sight.

"Nothing to worry about," Carl whispered back. Mort didn't get distracted easily, but it never hurt to be cautious. "We just do astral drive the old-fashioned way around here."

"I mean on the floor."

Carl shrugged. "Glyphs. Mort knows what they all do; ask him when he's done if you want to know."

Adam nodded absently, still staring at Mort.

When the chant ended, the glow in the glyphs faded and disappeared. Mort slouched down with a sigh and headed back to his quarters with the staff. "I need a nap."

"How deep did you put us?" Carl asked. While the thrusters of the *Mobius* could send them in any direction through real space, it took wizardry to move perpendicular to reality. Wizards had dubbed the region where space compressed the "astral plane," and the deeper a ship went, the faster it traveled relative to normal space. There were industry and guild standards that kept astral drive users slotted into standard depths, forming "lanes" and keeping communication and rescue efforts organized.

Mort just pointed over his shoulder at the speaker for the comm. A few seconds later, as Mort left the room, it crackled with Tanny's voice from the cockpit. "We're at a depth of six point eight, two, two and holding. Is Mort done?"

Carl hit the comm button with the butt of his fist. "Yeah, he's going to nap it off. We're good to go."

"Soon as I convince the nav computer that this depth is legit, we'll get underway. We should be at Willamette Station in a little over three hours."

Adam's head snapped up. "How's that possible? It should be days from here."

Carl gave the boy a sidelong glance. "You some expert on

astral travel?" he asked with a chuckle. "We don't keep Mort around for his personality."

The Kearny system was just outside of what ARGO officially claimed as protected territory. None of the worlds were inhabited, but three of them showed promise for future terraforming. Kearny III and Kearny IV were two planets in the habitable zone with liquid water but no breathable atmosphere. The only ones living there were part of tiny colonies dedicated to scientific research. Set in a solar orbit between the two was Willamette Station. It was a floating outpost of commerce and civilization amid the lifeless system.

It also looked like a scrapyard that had developed its own gravity. There was no grand plan for the station's layout or architecture. It had been founded when a pre-fab orbital habitat was hijacked by pirates and placed in orbit in the system. From there, it expanded when opportunistic businessmen convinced the owners that it could make money as a fueling station, then as a supply depot, and later as a refuge for those looking to do their business free from the overbearing eyes of ARGO patrols. Earth Navy designated the station and the surrounding system as lawless, but Willamette Station had plenty of rules.

Tanny guided the *Mobius* into the hangar they'd been assigned by Willamette traffic control. A faint blue haze parted for them as the ship pushed through the air lock force field. Dingy yellow overheads gave the hangar bay a sickly look, but the structure appeared solid. As they set down with a soft thump, barely noticeable due to the ship's gravity compensator, a set of doors slid into place to cover the air lock. Carl hated in-hangar berths on space stations for that reason; watching from the cockpit, it made him feel like his ship was being devoured.

"We're secured," Roddy's voice came over the comm.

Carl keyed the ship-wide comm. "We're down, everyone. Enjoy the amenities while we're here, but be back by oh-nine-hundred ship time tomorrow."

On his way down to the cargo hold, he nearly ran into Esper and Adam. Pulling up short of the startled former priestess, he stuck out his hand. "Nice having you aboard. Good luck with the kid." He tousled Adam's hair, which prompted a flinch and a grimace from the boy. "You take good care of her, too. I find out you given her any trouble, I'll sic Mriy on you." He winked, in case Adam couldn't tell he was joking.

The cargo bay door was open when Carl arrived. Roddy had just finished loading crates with their haul onto an anti-grav sled. It was too quick a job for Carl's liking. A few pulsed computer cores and an assortment of semi-valuable personal effects weren't much to refuel a starship on. He just hoped he could get enough for the escape pod to make up for the damage to the transport's computers. They were leaving the pod in the ship, because it was either that or leave everything else behind; it would have taken the whole anti-grav sled to haul it. It was easy enough to describe to anyone who'd buy that sort of thing.

"Hop on," Roddy said, jerking the thumb of his right foot toward the passenger seat.

Carl climbed aboard, smiling ruefully that no one even let him drive a grav sled—not that he'd have wanted to. It was just the principle of the matter. The sled sagged momentarily under Carl's weight before it readjusted to the imbalance, but never came back fully level. "Shitty rentals. We should buy one of our own one of these days."

"Maybe you should stick to vegetables," Roddy replied. "Your species isn't cut out to be omnivorous."

"It's not me; it's the sled!"

Roddy shook his head and cracked open a can of beer. "You

keep telling yourself that." The sled needed just two hands to drive, and that left Roddy free to drink and pilot at the same time.

The sled whizzed past the rest of the crew as they disembarked, and Carl held up a hand to wave. Esper noticed and raised a hand in reply. Adam just stood with his arms folded and his jaw set, eyes scanning the landing zone. There seemed something shrewd in the look, but Carl passed the notion off as the work of his imagination baiting his natural paranoia.

Tanny and Mriy would probably be off to find a holo-relay to watch—something with a bigger viewer than the *Mobius* boasted, and with new vids in from civilized space. If he was lucky, they'd poke around for a job while they were out. Mort would stay in the ship; Willamette Station wasn't the sort of place that appreciated wizards. It was self-contained, fully sci-dependent for life support, with no outside atmosphere to fall back on. A magic-related mishap was the last thing anyone aboard wanted.

He hoped Esper and Adam managed to find a cheap ride back to ARGO space, but it didn't seem likely. One of the downsides of living outside civilized space was that people charge extra to take you to and from it. They'd claim it was because of security worries, or because of concerns over having a passenger who was the sort who dealt outside the law, but it mostly came down to supply and demand. There weren't a thousand transports leaving every hour, like the Earth-Mars shuttle service. Ten departures taking passengers might be a good day, and that was if you weren't picky about getting to your destination directly.

"They'll be fine," Roddy said, catching Carl looking back.

"How can you be sure?"

Roddy chuckled. "They survived being with us. It's all autopilot for them from here."

Sprokytz was a typical junker. The equipment was all franchise-bought, the decor gaudy, with too many flashing lights and over-saturated colors. The three laakus working behind the counter passed items from one to the next, turning them over and examining each in detail. They muttered to one another in low voices, cognizant that Carl could understand their language—and of course, Roddy was one of their own kind. Outside in what passed for a road within Willamette station, two more laaku techs scanned the computer cores.

Carl browsed the shelves, daring any part of the oddball collection to catch his eye. A set of analog binoculars. A few well-worn kids' toys. A datapad twenty years out of date. A little statue of someone's idea of a well-endowed frog. Crap, the lot of it. Roddy was at the inventory kiosk, poking through the ship equipment Sprokytz kept in the warehouse.

"Anything worthwhile?" Carl asked, looking over Roddy's shoulder. He had to bend down, since the screen was placed at a height that was a compromise between human ergonomic standard and laaku common accommodation.

Roddy didn't look up. "I could build us a new ship from this stuff."

"Anything we can afford?"

"Not unless you've been holding out on us," Roddy replied.

"I wish," Carl said, eyes drawn to the 2D image of a pair of XK-80 ion thrusters with fifty percent higher power output than the *Mobius's* main engines. They were meant for an in-system racer, but that sort of detail had never stopped Roddy before. The *Mobius* was a testament to his ability to force disparate components into a working vessel.

Roddy cleared his throat. "You know, I never saw Chip spending much of his own share ..."

Carl gave him a dirty look. "And you never saw him digitize it as fast as he earned it? You know he didn't trust hard currency."

"Well, maybe if you ... or maybe Tanny happened to know his encryption code ..."

"Even if I did, I'm not robbing my own crew," Carl replied. "That money goes to his family ... assuming anyone can even get at it. He never left *me* any codes."

"Tanny's his cousin."

"Just drop it."

Roddy sighed, looking longingly at the XK-80 ion engines. "That pile of shit we brought in won't come close."

"Maybe with the escape pod," Carl said. "It's in perfect working order. That's gotta be rare as rain around here."

Jekjo walked in from inspecting the computer cores. The laaku wiped an upper hand on his coveralls to clean away some of the grime and offered it to Carl. "Thanks for stopping by," he said as he and Carl shook. Of all the non-terrestrial races, the laakus had most thoroughly adapted to live according to human norms. They learned Earth Standard English in primary school, watched human-made holos, and generally tried to act as human as their physiology allowed. Jekjo and his gang were old-fashioned, living outside ARGO space and keeping the old language, but Earth had rubbed off on them anyway.

"What're you going to give me for the lot?" Carl asked.

Jekjo looked to his crew behind the counter. A series of looks and subtle gestures passed between them. Carl didn't bother trying to puzzle any of it out; it was their own signaling system. Carl exchanged a look of his own with Roddy, and didn't like what he saw. Roddy could read Jekjo's body language better than he could, and Carl could already feel the pain in his bank account. He was disappointed before Jekjo even came back with a number.

"Eight hundred for the personals, thirty five for the cores," Jejko pronounced after the conference concluded.

Carl's eyes shot wide. "You can't be serious. I was upfront

about the cores being blanked; you don't have to put the screws to me over it. Those are worth at least five-k to you."

"I'm being generous on the personals because I like you, Carl," Jekjo replied, lifting his hands in a helpless gesture. "You bring me stuff I can turn around pretty easy most times. This lot though ... it's a dud."

"I also got an escape pod, came through in good shape, just needs a recharge on the life support." Carl had hoped the pod would be icing on the cake. Now, he was just hoping to eat the icing.

"You said that it was a Berring class passenger transport?" Jekjo asked. Carl nodded, and Jekjo laughed. "There's more escape pods for those heaps than you could ever fit onto the working ships. Those things are death traps. That thing'd be taking up space in my warehouse for years."

"Someone could use it for a refit," Roddy suggested.

Jekjo ignored him, and Carl felt a brief pang for his friend. Roddy did better dealing with laakus who didn't know him personally. "How much can you give me?" Carl asked, firing the thrust reversers on his expectations.

Jekjo shook his head. "I can shove the jewelry and knick-knacks on a shelf and let them take up space, but I can't afford to waste the room a worthless escape pod will take up. Can't do it."

"Rryzgat!" Carl swore, continually amused that his translator charm never converted the curses Mriy had taught him from her language. It certainly gave its best effort when he heard her use them.

"What's that?" Jekjo asked, narrowing his simian eyes.

"Nothing," Roddy said. "We'll take the forty-three hundred for the lot."

Jekjo picked at something in his teeth as he sized them up. "OK. You've got yourself a—"

"What if we threw in the grav sled?" Carl asked. Forty-three hundred was cutting things close. Even splitting things one fewer way, the ship's share plus his own was barely going to cover fuel.

Roddy shot Carl a panicked look, which Carl pretended not to notice.

"That's a rental," Jekjo said with a frown.

"Bought it refurb," Carl replied. "Got sick of renting one in every port. Figured I'd save a few terras having my own."

Jekjo exchanged some gestures with his gang behind the counter, who had kept a respectful vigil as their boss negotiated. "I assume you've got documentation to back that up?" Jekjo asked.

Carl grinned. "Of course not. Same as you, I don't keep anything on file that I don't have to produce for an ARGO inspection."

Jekjo stared at him for a moment. Carl could imagine the math at work in the laaku's head. They both knew it was theft, but on a station the size of Willamette, it was something that could get done. Jekjo could sit on the sled until Dynamik Transport wrote it off and forgot the whole matter; Carl would steer clear of the Kearny system for a while.

"I'll give you thirteen thousand for it," Jekjo offered. The crew behind the counter bobbed their heads in concurrence.

"Fifteen," Carl countered.

Jekjo scowled. "Why can't you people ever take an offer at face value?"

"Because I know you take the haggling into account. Besides, you'll turn it around for a solid thirty."

"Fine. That's ninety thousand eight hundred," Jekjo said. He stuck out a hand again and Carl shook it.

"Hard cash, of course," Carl said with a wink.

They returned to the *Mobius* on foot, picking their way through the crowds on the pedestrian overpasses as anti-grav vehicles sped by beneath. The smells from the restaurants tugged at Carl's stomach, begging him to enter with scents of grilled meats and fresh bread. But there was a heap of money in his pocket, most of it belonging to his crew, and Carl felt the weight of it sagging his pockets. He needed to get back to the ship and at least stow Tanny, Mort, and Mriy's shares. Roddy insisted on skimming his cut before they left the Sprokytz.

"You know we lose our deposit on that grav-sled," Roddy reminded him.

"Yup."

"You know we're in a heap of trouble when we leave port without returning it," Roddy added.

Carl shrugged. "We report it stolen, we apologize ... they'll get over it."

"What're we gonna do with that damn escape pod? Air-lock it once we get out of system?"

"Nah," Carl replied. "We'll keep trying. Someone's bound to take it off our hands."

As they approached the *Mobius*, they saw Esper pacing the hangar outside. She was still dressed in the clothes she had taken from the haul; Carl had assumed a clothing store would have been one of her first stops. She was wringing her hands and watching the entrance. When Carl and Roddy approached she perked up instantly.

"He's gone!" she said. She hurried over to intercept Carl. "I don't know what to do."

Carl shrugged. "He's got to be around somewhere. He'll turn up. Have you considered asking the local cops? They're not the most pleasant bunch, but they oughta have a soft spot for a lost kid."

Esper pursed her lips and frowned. "I'm not his legal guardian. I can't get help from anyone official ..."

"She's right on that one," Roddy said. "They'll probably think she's after a bounty."

Carl snickered and glanced up and down the wispy priestess. "Her?"

"Some of 'em are pretty good actors," said Roddy, wagging a finger.

"Well, what do you expect us to do?" Carl asked. "We're not cops. Hire someone local to help you."

"I don't know anyone local," Esper protested. "Everyone seems so ... sinful. I don't know who to trust. You treated me and Adam like guests."

"I guess by local standards, we *are* pretty respectable," said Roddy.

Carl cast him a sidelong we-just-sold-a-rented-grav-sled look, and Roddy gave a subtle shrug in reply.

"I imagine his parents can reward you if you help me get him home," Esper said. She looked at Carl with such pleading hope in her eyes.

Carl sighed, his resolve no match for a girl in trouble. "Fine. Lemme get Tanny and Mriy on the comm." He pulled out his pocket comm link. "Hey, why didn't you ask Mort to help? You wouldn't have had to wait outside for us."

"I'm a little afraid of Mort."

Roddy's shoulders shook in a silent chuckle.

Carl spoke into his comm. "Tanny, are you with Mriy? ... good, get back to the *Mobius* ... yeah, it's urgent ... Adam's missing ... yes, I agreed already." He flicked the comm off. "They're on their way."

Carl and Tanny jostled their way through the crowds of Willamette Station, past noodle shops and tattoo parlors, palm readers and black market drug smugglers with their own store fronts, courier services and holo-vid parlors. It wasn't the sort of place most people brought children, especially not their own. The ones who did were mostly hardened sorts, the ones that didn't expect anything more from their offspring than to take over the reins of their own ill-won criminal enterprises. Adam ought to have stood out like a puppy in a pigsty.

"Have you seen my nephew?" Carl asked a clean-cut man in a navy surplus coat. "Ten years old, light brown hair, about yeah high."

The man in the navy coat jerked back like Carl had a skin condition that looked contagious. "Human?" he asked.

"Of course he's human, gene-spliced mule, what do I look— never mind."

Carl took Tanny by the hand and led her away. They were posing as husband and wife, a micron-thin cover identity that she hated, but agreed to in order not to raise suspicion when looking for a child. Her grip just about cut off circulation to Carl's fingers, warning him that he was getting too close to his cover story.

Tanny flagged down a young couple who seemed like they might prove sympathetic. "We're looking for a lost boy: human, ten, skinny with brown hair. Have you seen him?"

They looked at one another. "I think so," the woman said. "Blue eyes?"

Tanny froze. Carl bit the inside of his cheek to keep from crying out at the pain in his hand as she tightened her grip reflexively. "Uh, yeah."

"I saw him with a couple mercs in body armor," the woman said. "I think maybe they're station security. I couldn't say for sure; this is our first time outside ARGO space. Isn't it exciting?" She smiled, revealing all gold teeth—body-mod fanatic. When

Carl looked closer, he noticed that her ears were slit to look like flower petals, and there were diamonds set into the whites of her eyes.

"Thanks," Tanny said. She let go of Carl's hand and headed off. Carl rushed to keep up with her before she disappeared into the crowd. His hand tingled as blood returned to its normal flow.

"Where you going?"

"Hangars," Tanny replied. "Willamette doesn't hire mercs; everyone's uniformed who works for the station."

Esper followed close behind Mriy, thankful that someone else was clearing a path for her. She had grown unaccustomed to crowds. The Harmony Bay settlement on Bentus VIII had been wide open. There was none of the forced closeness resulting from having a fully artificial atmosphere; the planet was designated Earth-like, and she could go outside and see clouds and birds in the sky. Aboard Willamette Station, everyone fought for enough room to breathe. But nobody got in Mriy's way. Strange xenos were usually given a wide berth, just as a general precaution. Anyone familiar with the azrin race would have kept even farther from her path.

There had been little to do aboard the *Mobius*, so among other things, Esper had looked up whatever she could find on Mriy's people. Despite being bipedal, they were evolved from her world's equivalent of tigers and lions and house cats. There was no direct correlation to Earth species. They weren't a technological people, only discovering space flight by having human explorers land on their world and explain the concept at gunpoint. They were an ARGO protectorate, not actual members, and most of their population preferred to live on-world.

Those that left usually worked grunt jobs in personal security or mercenary companies.

Knowing all this, Esper had mixed feelings about enlisting Mriy in the search for Adam. "You sure this is a good idea?" she asked Roddy quietly.

Roddy plodded along in Esper's wake, just as Esper used Mriy to clear a path for her. "Sure, why not? She likes the kid. She catches a whiff of him, we'll have him back in no time."

Mriy garbled something, but Esper had no magic earring to tell her what the azrin was saying. She looked to Roddy, who gave a long-suffering sigh. "She says she'll find the little warrior." He beckoned for Esper to lean close, so he could whisper. "I think she figures the fighting games are a sign he's got a vicious streak."

Esper nodded, wondering if there was any truth to it. Adam had never struck her as violent, but he was an excitable boy and seemed competitive.

Suddenly, Mriy stopped in the middle of the pedestrian walkway. Esper bumped into her from behind, but the azrin didn't seem to notice or care. She growled something, and her head snapped to the left.

"She's found him," Roddy said. "Or at least a scent."

"What are we waiting for?" Esper asked. "Let's go."

Mriy said something else. "She wants you to stay behind. Meet us at the ship. She'll handle it from here."

Esper drew herself up tall. "I most certainly will not! He's my responsibility, and I'm the one he'll be hoping to see."

Mriy nodded. That needed no translation.

They plowed through the crowd, Mriy's snarling demeanor keeping station-goers from hindering them. The azrin danced the tight line between efficient bullying and getting station security summoned to arrest them. They left the commercial district where they began their search, and continued into the maintenance bays, station subsystem access points, and finally to the far end of the hangars from where the *Mobius* was berthed. Mriy pointed a palm at one of the personnel doors.

"This is the place," said Roddy.

Esper's heart raced. If they had gotten to him, he could already be aboard a ship back to Harmony Bay. "Open it!"

"You keep back," Roddy said.

Mriy shoved the door open and stalked through. Inside, a sleek, modern interceptor ship sat with its cargo bay door open. Metallic crates lined the wall, some of them still on the grav-sled that had brought them. Two mercenaries in glistening black body armor stood over the merchandise, one reading from a datapad, the other poking through the crates' contents. Their helmets were perched on the seats of the grav sled.

"Hey, what're you doing in—?" one of them began to ask.

"They must be after the kid," the other one cut in. The datapad clattered to the floor, and both mercenaries grabbed for their helmets. Mriy growled something that Roddy didn't bother to translate, and both men drew clubs from hooks on their belts. Esper hadn't actually gotten around to reading the station rules, so she wasn't sure how lax they were on weapons inside a rented hangar bay. The clubs looked like metallized plastic, and there was a device built into the end of each.

"Just give us Adam and no one needs to get hurt," Esper shouted, seeing the conflict about to play out in front of her.

"We got a job to do, ma'am. We ain't handing that boy over to you or anyone else," the mercenary who dropped the datapad replied. "Maybe you just want to call off your cat, and let us do our job."

Mriy's natural slouch made her appear short by human standards, but physiology is a strange thing. As she snarled in defiance, she drew herself up to her full, two-meter height, towering over both mercenaries. The mercenaries exchanged a look from behind the black, featureless helmets, then looked back to Mriy.

They spread out and came at Mriy from the sides. Crackling blue arcs snapped at the clubs' ends as they swung toward the azrin.

But neither had ever fought an azrin; that much was plain to see. She caught first one, then the other by the wrist, her own arms moving faster than any human could react without cybernetic limbs. She twisted her right wrist, and the mercenary in her grasp dropped his stun club. She yanked on the mercenary to her right, lifting him as she drew him close, and tore his throat out with her teeth, forcing her way beneath the helmet. Dropping the body, she extended her claws and slashed out the throat of the other.

The whole encounter took perhaps five seconds.

Esper swallowed. She clasped her hands together to stop them shaking, and found herself in need of prayer. "I run to you, Lord ..."

"Yeah, she has that effect on me sometimes, too," said Roddy. "But let's go check the ship for the kid."

"This should be it: hangar eighty-four" Carl said, huffing for breath. They had crossed the full length of the station to reach their destination, the hangar that three witnesses had identified. If the two armored figures with him were the kidnappers, this is where their ship was berthed.

"We should have brought a weapon," Tanny said, putting a hand to the door controls.

"*Praesertim virtute*, right?" Carl asked with a smile. The translator charm didn't correct his Latin either.

Tanny frowned at him quoting the marines' motto back at her. She hammered the door controls with a fist and burst inside. Even unarmed, Carl liked her odds against two flash-and-polish mercenaries. No one walked around a space station in armor unless they were assaulting it, or they needed people to think they were bigger badasses than they really were.

Carl poked his head in after giving himself a five-count. There had been no signs of trouble, just the sound of Tanny's boots on the steel plates of the floor, but even those had stopped. What he saw was Tanny staring back at him with her arms crossed and a scowl on her face. He also saw Mriy and Roddy by the cargo ramp of the mercenaries' interceptor, two dead bodies, and his erstwhile passengers. With a shrug of apology to his ex-wife, Carl strolled into the hangar, checking over his shoulder as he closed the door behind him.

"Well, it looks like you all made quite a mess in here," Carl remarked, giving a slight frown. It was the same look his commanding officers used to use when inspecting something and needing to make up a flaw for the sake of feeling useful. "Lucky for you, I think I see how to fix this. By the by, you all right, kid?"

Adam nodded.

"I think we have to let the authorities know what happened here," Esper said.

"Um—" "Yeah, maybe not—" "I see no reason—"

Carl just smiled and held up his hands. "No need to be hasty. This sort of misunderstanding happens in places like this. We just need to make sure no one gets sore at *us* until we're a few systems away. Mriy, thanks for taking care of those two." Mriy grinned, showing her fangs. "Now, drag that mess you made into their ship and dump them in the crew quarters." Her grin turned into a hiss. "Oh, and clean up when you're done. You've still got a bit of human ... right ..." Carl pointed a finger to a spot on his cheek, and mirrored Mriy until she found the spot on her own cheek that was still bloody.

"You want me to check if they had surveillance on the hangar?" Roddy asked.

"Station won't—that sort of snooping's bad for business—but

you can check the ship," said Carl. "Pocket anything you see that you like."

"I'll get Esper and Adam back to the ship," Tanny volunteered.

Carl's eyes drifted over to the anti-grav sled parked to the side of the hangar. A mischievous grin betrayed his idea even before he said a word. "Not yet. Help me load up that sled."

"We can't afford to waste time stealing a grav sled," Tanny argued.

As he climbed the cargo ramp, Roddy stuck his head back down. "Well, he sold the one we rented, so maybe a replacement isn't a bad idea."

"You're kidding me."

"The cut'll drop from thirty-three hundred to under three grand if we don't get our deposit back," said Roddy. "I'm not a charity."

"You can't just—" Esper began.

"Let's get this thing loaded," Tanny barked. Adam snapped to attention like a raw recruit and pitched in. Carl and Tanny started heaving crates back onto the grav sled without even looking. Noticing the datapad on the floor, Carl tucked it between two of the crates.

Esper looked on with a helpless, horrified expression.

"Mind giving us a hand?" Carl asked. "This'll go quicker, and we'll get out of here."

"I can't ..."

"Listen, Sister," Carl said. "We just ended up with a double-homicide grabbing Adam back for you. Maybe if they investigate, we'll get our names cleared. More than likely, they'll dust us just to keep their law-and-order reputation appearances up. Now, grab a crate and pitch in."

Two hours later, the *Mobius* was deep in the astral again, leaving Willamette Station behind—possibly for good. Mort had put them shallow this time, letting them have the time to think about their next move. Something wasn't sitting well with Carl, a nagging thought buzzing in the back of his brain. He needed some time to think, to throw ideas in a heap, sort them into piles, then kick the piles over and start again. Esper and Adam were back in Chip's old quarters as if the *Mobius* had never offloaded them. Tanny was at the controls, probably reading. Mriy and Roddy were in the hold, sorting through the mercenaries' cargo. That left Mort.

Digging through his quarters, Carl found a battered cardboard box with lettering too faded to read anymore. He gave it a cursory dusting with a shirtsleeve, and headed up to the common room. The box was older than Carl or even Carl's parents. It had belonged to his grandfather, and it had been passed down through the generations. One day, Carl was going to have to find a new box to replace it, but until it crumbled to confetti, he was going to keep using the original packaging. Carl removed a plastic housing, three hundred centimeters on a side, and placed it on the kitchen table. Tucked beneath it were two stacks of composite plastic datacards, each bundled together with an elastic band. Glancing at the two bundles, Carl set one down across the table from him, and removed the elastic from the other.

"Mort," he called out, loudly enough for the wizard to hear from his quarters. "Up for a game of Battle Minions?" There was a chronometer on the common room wall, set to Greenwich Mean Time. Carl watched the seconds blip by.

Eight seconds later, Mort's door opened. "You're what now?"

"Come on, it's been weeks," Carl said. "I still owe you one from last time." He flipped through his stack of minions, trying to decide how best to prepare for facing Mort's.

Mort stopped by the refrigerator and pulled out a pair of

beers. He tossed one to Carl and the other opened of its own accord in his hand.

"Watch it," Carl chided him, not for throwing the can, but for magicking his own open. "I actually want to *play* a game, not spend hours trying to log into the omni from a random depth to restore our minion data."

Mort waved away Carl's concerns as he took a sip of his beer. "I'm careful. So, what're you in the mood for? Standard game, gladiator, or one of those flaky custom setups you keep pestering me about?"

"Just standard," Carl said as Mort unbound his minion datacards. "I need to talk something over with you."

Mort squinted one eye at Carl, a look that sent some men clutching for charms of protection. Carl had seen it too many times, and just smirked back. "Tanny trouble again, or something with those two?" Mort asked, pointing with his nose in the direction of Esper and Adam's temporary quarters.

"The kid," Carl confirmed. He finished his selection of minions and fed the eight chosen datacards into his side of the game board. "Something just seems off with him. You talk with him much? I see you two gaming enough."

"Enough, I suppose," Mort replied. "Nice kid. Got his head on straight. Miracle after what they probably did to him."

"He doesn't seem ... I don't know ... a little phony?"

"I'm no expert on kids, but I'm a fair judge of minds. Don't know what the scientists did to the kids at that school the plastic girl taught at, but the teachers have done well by him. Politics, religion, music, he's got a pretty broad set of interests."

"And you two just sit around playing Omnithrust Racer, talking politics?" Carl asked.

"Adam and I see eye-to-eye on the Mitchell Administration, AGRO membership expansion, and Earth preservation. He's a bit too pro-science for my liking, but I blame the schools for that."

"I'll let Esper know you disapprove of her curriculum," Carl joked.

"Bah, she taught math," Mort replied. "Best thing I can say about her, really. The One Church's 'magic for Him, not for you' stance sours the lot of them." Mort slid his own minions into the machine and the game began. Little holographic monsters rose from the game board and sized each other up. Carl and Mort keyed in last-second modifications to their minions' orders as a holographic clock counted down seconds until the battle started.

The two of them watched the battle unfold. The cherubic, colorful creatures with their absurd and oft impractical-looking weapons clashed in the middle of the board. They grunted and squished as they attempted to hack one another to pieces. Carl's squad was big and brutish, and tried to occupy the center of the battlefield. Mort's squad spread out and picked at the edges of Carl's defenses. There was nothing to do but watch and wait, as the commands were preset prior to the game's beginning.

"Come on ... come on ..." Carl breathed, clenching his fists. Every creature of his was stronger and tougher than any of Mort's, yet Mort was gaining the upper hand. When the last of Carl's minions expired with a melodramatic "Euuuaaa!", the game played a happy little tune and pronounced Mort the winner.

The old wizard chuckled. "You try that plan every few battles you know. All big dumb brutes just doesn't work against a competent opponent."

Carl tipped back in his chair and sighed. "I just wanted something straightforward to work for once. Why does everything need to be complicated?"

Mort twisted his lips; it was a facial shrug, as far as Carl could tell. "Just the way the universe works. You got no business complaining; you think you got where you are today by playing it straight?"

"I know. I know. I just feel like I deserve a break now and then," Carl said. "Something with someone shooting at me, and I can shoot back ... not that I want to get shot."

"Navy's always recruiting," Mort said with a grin.

Carl yanked his datacards out of the game board and began sorting through them. "Yeah, and have them put me back on Earth, teaching twitchy teenagers how to fly? And another thing, how'd I end up playing ferry to those two again? I've never taken a job with such a sketchy payout."

"You'd just gotten short-ended on our last haul, plus a few glandular inconveniences clouding your thinking."

"She's not my type," Carl replied.

Mort snickered. "Dark science or no, she's any man's type who hasn't got himself situated. Plus, there's Adam. Man can't feel like a proper man if he can't look after a kid."

"Even if the kid's comet cold when you rescue him? Mort, I tell you, the kid's not right in the head. You'd think we picked him up from school, not a kidnapping."

Mort shook his head. "Dark science, my boy. It's not pretty. Speaking of which, you should go talk to her and get it out of your system. Oh, and if you want the boy out of the room for say ... an hour or two, just tell him I wanted to try Neptune Squad."

"You're incorrigible."

"Why would I want to be corriged?" Mort asked with a wink.

Carl knocked softly on the door to Chip's old quarters, wondering how long it would be until he stopped thinking of it as Chip's. Since each of the crew quarters on the *Mobius* was a separate escape pod, it was possible he could just trade it in for a new one; Carl had been thinking a lot about what to do with escape pods of late. It was a shame that the one in the cargo hold was incompatible. Even Roddy was unlikely to be able to force it to fit.

There was no answer from inside, and Carl had lifted his knuckles to knock louder when the door opened. Esper peeked out before opening the door wider to let Carl inside. "Captain?" she whispered. Adam was sleeping on Chip's bed, still dressed with shoes and everything, on top of the blankets.

"Yeah, thought he might be sleeping it off," Carl whispered back. "Rough day. Can you join me ..." Carl paused. He was about to suggest his quarters, but with Mort's teasing fresh in his mind, he changed his course. "... down in the cargo hold? We need to talk."

Esper didn't question him, but followed Carl up the stairs and through the common room. Mort gave a disapproving scowl as he fought with the holovid controls, but said nothing. Down in the cargo hold, Roddy and Mriy were prying and cutting the lids off the stolen crates, many of which were sealed shut. They both looked up at the sound of footsteps on the landing.

"You two take a break," Carl called down as he descended. "Give Mort a hand with the holovid and find something to watch."

"C'mon, we were just getting to the fun part," Roddy griped. "These Grayson & Wesson locks took forever to bust open."

Mriy nodded in agreement. "Go mate in your own quarters."

"What'd she say?" Esper asked quietly.

"She wants to see what we got," Carl lied softly, "same as Roddy." He got down to the cargo floor and peered over Roddy to see what they were excited about. "What *do* we have?"

"Manifest's encrypted, so we only know as we open them," Roddy said. He lifted the lid on one with a lower hand. "This one's just a sniff of the ion trail." Inside, there was a rack of disintegrator rifles, UniDef Systems' Adjudicator Mk VII series.

Carl let out a low whistle. "That crate's worth almost as much as this ship."

Roddy snorted. "Sure, and anyone missing a shipment of these babies gets word we boosted them, we're not just dusted, we're particles."

"Problem for later," Carl replied. "Now, go grab a beer and watch some *Samolith* or something with Mort."

"The Tri-Annual Hunt might be on relay," Mriy said.

Carl held up his hands and ushered Mriy and Roddy toward the stairs. "Whatever the three of you can agree on. Hell, grab Tanny and make a party of it; not like there's much to watch for in the shallow astral. Just get a move on."

Roddy fixed Carl with a glare and a meaningful look at the crates as he departed, adding the rubbing fingers gesture humans used for "money."

Carl replied with a less couth gesture after making sure Esper wasn't looking.

"So what did you want to talk to me about?" she asked once the door to the main crew compartment closed.

Carl ran a hand through his hair as he tried to decide how to put it. It was odd: he could lie to a man with a gun pointed at his head, or a ship with its guns trained on the *Mobius* and never so much as stutter over his words. But the truth and a pretty pair of eyes looking back at him and he turned into a blathering idiot.

"It's Adam."

"Yes ... I've been thinking about him, too," Esper replied, crossing her arms. "I don't think I'm telling you where to bring him until we get to Mars. I don't trust you not to leave me stranded somewhere along the way if I tell you before then."

"You think I'm above knocking on two billion doors to get my reward?" Carl asked. He closed his eyes and shook his head; he couldn't afford to get pulled into a contest of clever one-upsmanship. "That's not the point. How did they find Adam?"

Esper blinked. "What do you mean?"

"How did they know he was on Willamette Station? We don't exactly publish an itinerary. The only ship that even knew we were in this sector was the Tally-ho."

"Maybe Harmony Bay has connections inside Earth Navy ..."

Carl pointed a finger at her. "Ah HA! I thought of that, but we hid Adam from them. I don't think those techs of Penny-Toad's were faking when they said they found nothing out of the ordinary. Mort fooled them good."

"Maybe they have scanners installed at all the starports ..."

"At every starport in the quadrant? Including Willamette Station, which isn't even in ARGO space? No, I'm thinking he might have a tracker planted in him."

Esper opened her mouth, aghast. "No, he can't. Doctor Cliffton said Adam's had been removed."

"That scientist who helped you smuggle him out?"

Esper nodded. "Doctor Cliffton got his doctorate from Oxford in cellular genetics. I don't think he'd miss something like that."

Carl nodded. It was time to dig into the background of Doctor Cliffton. "Well, we're going to get ourselves somewhere planetside and have Adam checked out. Nothing we've got on board is going to find a tracker if someone wanted it hidden."

"Wouldn't it be safer heading straight for Mars?" Esper asked.

Carl pinched his chin between thumb and forefinger, feeling the scruff of not having shaved in days. "Depends how good a tracker it is."

The descent into an unfamiliar atmosphere always put Carl a little on edge. Delos was the only habitable world in the system of the same name. The others got numbered and forgotten, but the fifth world from their sun was just Delos. It was a dry world on the Earth-like spectrum, with just a quarter of its surface covered in water. Most inhabitants of Earth didn't care for the weather, so the population centers were all domed in. The starport looked like a produce market, with pea-pod hangar bays, each berth having its own retractable hemisphere that split to allow entry and egress. Yet another landing point that wanted to eat his ship. One day, Carl figured he ought to talk to a professional about that imagery, before he went nuts (or as Tanny would have told him, any *more* nuts).

While most people still considered Delos to be the frontier, it was clean and safe compared to Willamette Station. Companies had corporate offices in places like Delos; whereas, the only organizations who sought out Willamette were the ones who didn't want the competition from legitimate businesses—or the oversight that went with it. One of the benefits of respectability was attracting doctors with valid medical licenses. You could get a hole patched up, or a parasite removed on just about any outpost. Delos had facilities that employed people who had done those sorts of things before, had gone to school to learn how, and had equipment designed just for that purpose. Carl still had a few scars from encounters with the other kind—sometimes you just had to take what you had available.

Their hangar was in the city of New Melbourne, one of the mid-sized settlements that dotted the sea of the southern hemisphere. While Delos catered to a mix of tourists and explorers, New Melbourne leaned toward the latter. Traders, cartographers, diplomats, smugglers, and pirates came and went from nearby xeno space; not many of the locals could tell them apart, and the smart ones just kept their heads down and counted the credits that flowed into their accounts.

As the crew filed down the loading ramp and into the hangar,

Carl doled out assignments, such as they were. "Tanny, you go with Esper and Adam. Make sure they get to the med facility without any trouble." Carl didn't need to spell out the sorts of trouble she needed to look for. Tanny was better qualified to identify those than he was. "Mriy ... just don't kill anyone while we're here. Mort, you can do whatever you feel like ... not like I could stop you anyway. Roddy, you and me are taking another shot at getting rid of that escape pod."

"Shit, Carl," said Roddy, "First real port in almost a month, and I'm stuck haggling with scrap dealers again?"

"I don't want them bullshitting me on tech details," said Carl. "I'll do the haggling."

"Yeah, but—"

"We'll find a good pub around here after. Drinks are on me," said Carl. "That goes for everyone."

New Melbourne Starport was bright and cheerful, with glossy white surfaces, colorful holovid displays showing departures and arrivals, and smiling personnel in teal uniforms. There were plenty of skylights looking up into the atmosphere as well, allowing bystanders to watch the ships taking off or landing. The glitz and polish were for the customers of the starliners; Carl and Roddy didn't see anything but utility corridors and cargo haulers until the private and commercial wings of the starport merged at the central hub.

"Look at the rubes," said Roddy, shaking his head. "All looking up, like they never saw a ship before."

"Maybe some of them haven't," Carl said. Looking around, it was the usual mix. Over ninety percent human, about half the rest Roddy's kind, and the other half a sprinkling of ARGO races. Nothing exotic. There wasn't even the typical vibe of a swagger and ego that came with a spacers' port. New Melbourne was tame, and Carl would have bet that there were people arriving by passenger liner that had never been outside the Terran system before.

As they walked the concourse, Roddy kept up a non-stop chatter. Sometimes he denigrated the false shine on everything in ARGO-secured space; other times he pointed out the people who weren't what they were dressed to be. Carl had heard it all before and auto-piloted some supportive responses to keep Roddy from demanding too much of his attention. Carl wanted to look in the shops. As with anyone possessed of a Y chromosome, he hated shopping unless it involved a device that converted power into forward motion, explosions, or entertainment. But he was fascinated looking through the windows of shops as they passed by. Most of the clothing stores catered to women's fashions and accessories. But there were also a number of shops hawking Delos-themed curios: shirts with images of the famous Angelic Falls, EV helms with the Delos "nine-planets, one Delos" logo and motto, and mugs boasting that the owner had flown the Zephyros Canyon Run. Other shops catered to basic necessities, perfunctory gifts, and personal entertainment.

Roddy's voice grew quieter and distant, petering away to nothing but the general hum of a thousand conversations bouncing around the concourse. Carl had stopped. Amid the coffee shops, sushi bars, and chain barbecue restaurants was one establishment that enveloped him, sight, sound, and soul: Duster's Dogfight Diner. They must have pumped something through the ventilation system, because amid the scents of grilled beef, fried chicken, and hot cakes, Carl smelled starfighter fuel rods. It was the largest restaurant they had seen on the concourse, and through the glass he could barely make out the giant holovid globe suspended above the patrons. Signs by the door didn't allow anyone to pass by without knowing what went on inside.

INTENSE STARFIGHTER ACTION!
FOUR-ON-FOUR TOURNEYS NIGHTLY!

CHAMPIONS EAT FREE!

NOT A PILOT? PLACE YOUR BETS ON THE ACTION!

Carl blinked when he felt a tug at his coat hem. Slowly, he returned to New Melbourne, the concourse, and his impending trip to find a salvage dealer. "Come on, flyboy," said Roddy. "If you wanna come back later, I'll drink anywhere."

"Yeah," Carl said, staring over his shoulder as Roddy towed him away from the diner. "Yeah, we'll come back later."

Carl sat on a molded plastic bench, meant to look and feel like stone. No matter how hard the chemists tried though, they could never make plastic feel *old* the way stone did. Real stone had a comforting eternal feel to it; it made your troubles seem fleeting and petty and helped put things in perspective. Carl had sat on real stone before, back on Earth, so he knew. Parked on a plastic bench next to a genetically perfect potted ficus tree, he felt the full weight of being at the mercy of a laaku's skill with the help kiosk. They had already tried every likely salvage yard within local tram distance and were back at the starport, looking to widen their search.

When Roddy returned, he was shaking his head. "I looked at other scrappers on Delos, and it's the same song. They'll melt it down for us for beer money. Starport's offer's as good as any. I say we just dump the thing and be done with it."

Carl stood up, shaking his head. "Naw, we've put too much effort into this to cut and run now. We'll hang onto it, maybe find a system running older transports and see if we can palm it off on them."

"It's really not worth the trouble, you know," Roddy said,

falling into step beside Carl as they headed back toward their hangar.

"Yeah, probably. Now it's a matter of principle, though."

"Principle doesn't pay."

Carl stuffed his hands into the pockets of his jacket. "I know, but principle's what keeps you going when the galaxy seems hell-bent on siphoning every terra out of your wallet."

"Come on," said Roddy. "Let's grab everyone and go out for that drink. That ought to cheer you up." Whether Roddy intended him to or not, Carl heard the muttered afterthought. "It'll sure cheer *me* up."

The lighting was low enough that the holovid globe could be seen from anywhere in the diner. Along two separate walls were banks of old flight simulator pods, four to a side. From those simulators, eight pilots controlled the action taking place above. Represented in the three-meter diameter globe was—according to displays built into the surface of each table—the Gespen Ship Graveyard, a man-made asteroid field of orbiting wrecks. Voice comm blared from overhead speakers, directionally oriented so that the knowledgeable observer could tell which team was talking.

Blue leader to Blue Two, you've picked up a tail.

Copy that Blue Leader, taking evasive.

"Noobs," Carl muttered, glaring longingly up at the holovid globe. The whole crew of the *Mobius* sat together at a round booth, along with Esper and Adam. The boy's scans had come back clear, and it looked like they had stopped at Delos for nothing but a bit of peace of mind.

"Shouldn't we be in the wizards' section?" Esper asked quietly. Anything below a shout was unlikely to be overheard. In addition to the comm chatter, bettors shouted encouragement to the teams they were backing, and a few beleaguered wait staff tried to run a restaurant.

"Young lady," said Mort. "It is a layman's misconception that wizards are inherently hazardous to scientific devices. It is the mark of a true wizard to refrain from magic at his will. I can—"

Tanny shushed him as the waiter with their drinks approached. He was dressed in a stylized Earth Navy cadet uniform, just obviously fake enough not to offend visiting naval personnel. Carl, Mort, Mriy, and Tanny had all ordered local Delos brews. Given limited options, Adam had requested a Cherry Hydro-Blaster. Esper went the safe route and ordered a caramel soda. For all his griping, Roddy just wanted Earth's preferred from the tap, which tasted hardly any different from the cans they kept aboard the *Mobius*.

"Well, so it turns out Adam's in fine health," Esper said, starting the conversation anew in a different direction.

Tanny shrugged, lifting the local approximation of an old Earth stout to her lips. "What would you expect from a lab rat?"

"I'm sitting right here," Adam protested.

"Hey kid, we all start somewhere," Tanny replied. "Not all of us are proud of where."

Viper Four, come about to two-six-oh mark one-five, and intercept.

Roger that, Viper One.

"Those guys aren't half bad," Carl remarked, staring up at the holovid globe. He absently tipped back his drink, never taking his eyes from the action.

"They're just little hologram flies buzzing around each other," said Esper. "How can you tell?"

"The blue squad's just faking it," Carl replied. "Bunch of passengers getting a chance to sit up front for once, and play-acting being pilots. They're flying around like cockroaches, not thinking, just reacting to their environment. The red team, the ones calling themselves Viper, is the real deal. I'd bet my take from our salvage job that these guys fly together."

Roddy snorted. "Big spender."

"No takers," Tanny added. "I can kind of see it, too. They either fly together, or they practically live in this joint."

"Pack hunters," Mriy agreed.

"So who's with me?"

They all looked to Carl.

"You didn't ..." said Tanny.

"We've got winner," said Carl. "It's going to be that Viper team. Look, they just went ahead by a ship. Anyway, I put Team Mobius on the list for tonight, but I need a roster. They'll come up with odds for us once I tell them who I'm flying with, and we see who we're facing."

"Can I?" asked Adam, looking to Esper, not Carl.

"Sure you can," Carl replied.

Tanny gave him a withering look. "You can't seriously think the kid can fly against those guys?"

"Think you can do better?" Carl asked. As soon as Tanny opened her mouth to reply, he cut her off. "Good, because I'm counting on you as my wingman."

Roddy held up his lower hands. "Don't look my way. Those human-sized cockpits are no place for me."

"Fair enough," Carl replied. "How about you, Esper?"

Esper choked on her drink, spluttering half a mouthful back into the glass.

"You OK?" Carl asked. "I was just joking. Come on, Mriy. It'll be like hunting, but without all the running and mess to clean up."

Mriy yawned and stretched, her arms spreading wide enough to span the whole table. "This looks better than the games on the ship."

As his squadron extracted themselves from the table, Carl

took advantage of the momentary distraction to lean in and whisper to Mort. "Bet everything you can scrape together on us. This'll make up for the scrawny haul."

Carl's eyes glazed over as the referee gave them instructions on both the battle setup and the basic controls of the simulator. He resisted the urge to tell the jumped-up waiter where he could shove his "new pilot tips," but he needed to keep his cool to let the odds drift up. Besides, Adam probably needed the help, possibly Mriy, too. Tanny would be fine. Piloting a marine transport wasn't like handling a starfighter, but she'd been through flight school—at least what the marines passed off as flight school.

As he climbed into the cockpit of the simulator labeled Blue Two, he felt a wave of nostalgia. Underneath the scent of beer and the rickety canopy whose hydraulics could have used an overhaul, it was still a Typhoon III simulator. It took Carl back to his academy days, not the first go-round as a cadet, but the second time, as a flight instructor teaching dirt-booted pilots how to fly the Typhoon IV. The differences between the two ships only mattered to sticklers and bureaucrats; it was even running the same UI and training programs.

Analog toggle switches were scattered across the inside of the cockpit. Without even giving it a second thought, Carl flipped through them in a standard pre-flight check. Most were stiff with disuse, a few sticky. It took Carl until he was halfway through the check before he noticed that none of them were functioning. Someone had dumbed down the simulator to diner-patron simplicity. The flight yoke was loose and free though, and had just the right amount of resistance to feel stable. Reaching behind him, he found the helm for Blue Two and plunked it down over his head with a grimace. He hadn't watched who had last flown in the unit, but now he smelled the foul chili-pepper concoction his predecessor had eaten prior to playing.

Once he had his helmet on, Carl was bombarded with comm noise.

This is great! We're going to win!

My ears are squashed against my head.

What'd she say?

Never mind.

All right, when we start, just follow my lead.

The comm was low-end and fuzzy and flattened the voices so badly that he could only tell the speakers by context. He should have realized that Adam wouldn't be able to understand Mriy. Mort could have loaned him his translator charm; the old wizard understood azrin well enough without it. In the end, of course, it didn't matter anyway. Let the diners laugh themselves silly until the fighting actually started.

Contrary to whatever instincts screamed in his head, Carl kept silent. The betting period would close once the simulated fighters launched. Hopefully Mort was letting the odds drift to their high point before placing his bet. It wouldn't have surprised him if Mort was the *only* one placing a bet on the Blue Squadron.

The heads-up display showed a countdown, starting thirty seconds out. Carl cracked his knuckles.

At twenty seconds, he tilted his neck back and forth, working loose any kinks.

At ten seconds, he took a long, slow breath.

Then the countdown hit zero. Carl punched the throttle to full and was first out of the simulated hangar. In flight school, it had always been a point to brag about. The simulators didn't accept any inputs before the countdown finished, so a partially opened throttle was a recipe for a slow start. His Typhoon III rocketed out into the hologlobe battlefield, which was different from the one the *Mobius* crew had just watched. Carl didn't need the nav display to know that it was Frontier Station Bravo, an unusual place for a dogfight. A working (albeit fictional) space station, Frontier Station Bravo was swarming with civilian traffic at the start of the simulation. In flight school runs, it was meant to be a defense against a raid, with the defense of the civilians paramount.

All right, everybody, you see them on radar? Let's get there before they know what hit them. Full throttle, and everyone aim for the guy on the far left. Adam's strategy was straight out of the pre-adolescent belief that heroes were bold and brave.

Mriy's ship followed as Adam continued to pour ions out of his thrusters, but Carl hung back, easing off his own throttle. Tanny was smart enough to follow suit. Shield flashes marked the opening salvos from both sides, Adam hitting several times from beyond his cannons' optimal range, and Mriy connecting once or twice with marginally effective shots. The Viper squad waited until they closed range with Adam and Mriy, and Blue Leader and Blue Four exploded in short order.

"Blue Two to Blue Three: Tanny, mind taking up position on my six. Let's show these guys some flying."

Roger Blue Two. Try not to get us both killed.

Carl laughed over the comm. "Don't worry; it's just a game." He opened the throttle and veered toward the civilian shipping lanes, where a thirty-four ship convoy was headed for the safety of the station's docking bays.

Carl, what are you doing?

The Viper Squadron turned to give chase, but their lines of fire were spoiled by congested ship traffic crossing between the two squads. Carl fought with an under-used switch on the side of the flight yoke, one not too many civilian sim-jockeys would bother with even if they realized it was there. He flicked it on and off, working the switch loose, the simulator's hydraulics bucking to mimic the shuddering that alternating the flight control assist on and off would cause. He left it in the "off" position and pivoted his typhoon to aim the guns back at Viper Squadron. Starfighters were complicated enough to fly without needing to perform advanced physics calculations on the go. The flight control system made the ship compensate for existing momentum in executing turns and rolls. With it turned off, Carl had the freedom to spin his ship and fire his lateral and vertical thrusters to angle in any direction he liked—but he had to worry about managing the ship's momentum himself.

Of course, now he was flying mostly backwards and a bit to port.

Tanny dove out of his way as Carl opened fire. He tracked one of the Viper Squad, shooting it just before it passed behind a medical evac ship, then again once it emerged on the far side. The target's shields sputtered and died out, as Carl's shot hit at the spot where the generator was most vulnerable. Tanny swung around and put in two quick shots to destroy it.

"Nice shooting."

"You're a fucking maniac!"

Carl grinned, turning his flight controls back on and slinging his ship through the station traffic. He headed for the far side of the station, Tanny taking up position behind him.

"Where are we going? They're the other way."

"I'm a good shot, but there's still three of them. Rather string 'em out and pick 'em off."

The station's defense cannons fired, but it was all for show. Unless someone had really monkeyed with the programming, they would never aim anywhere near the combatants. They were just meant to make cadets feel like they were in a live-fire situation. Avoiding a fleeing passenger liner, Carl swung through the interior of the ring-shaped station. Checking his radar, he saw that the three remaining members of Viper Squadron were closing in, spread wide to take up multiple firing angles.

As soon as he broke line-of-sight with them, Carl switched off the flight assist again and spun his typhoon.

Stop doing that!

Tanny looped around in a standard turn, but didn't have her guns around by the time Carl opened fire on the first of the Vipers to emerge from behind the station's bulk. Using his vertical thrusters and pitching downward simultaneously, he maneuvered his craft to keep its aim on the Vipers while backing out of the path of their turn to intercept him. One exploded in a hail of withering fire from Carl's cannons, but the other two changed tactics and focused their fire on Tanny. Her long, looping turn had left her exposed with nothing but her shields between her and the two Vipers. Twisting and rolling, she tried to keep them off target, but she was blasted out of space.

Carl found himself alone against two opponents. He breathed a sigh of relief, careful not to have his comm open. With a growing grin, he fired his directional thrusters and looped around to give chase.

There were any number of ways that flight school cadets would react to unexpectedly finding themselves on the defensive. Carl had seen them all. The ones destined to wash out just panicked and froze. Others would scatter for cover, which was always a low-percentage play in deep space; not many real battles would take place in congested regions like the simulator. The good ones regrouped with their squadron and adapted to the flow of the fight. Carl had found a pair that wanted to go out in a blaze of glory; they both turned to fix their plasma cannons on his typhoon.

Carl turned on his comm and laughed out loud. He knew they couldn't hear him inside their simulator cockpits, but he taunted them anyway. "You lunar ferrymen couldn't hit your own mouths with a toothbrush. What are you even aiming at? Are you trying to blow up the station or me?"

Frontier Station Bravo had innumerable contours, from sensor arrays to small ship docking arms, gun ports to reactor nacelles. Carl knew them all as if he had built the place with his own two hands—not that it actually ever existed. He wove his way along the surface of the station with his ship's momentum carrying him along backward, firing his guns at the pursuing Vipers and using his thrusters to keep from crashing. It was a failing grade in any simulator run to splatter on an inanimate target, so he had always loved challenging cadets to chase him through the hazardous region.

"If you haven't already, can someone please set the display area to a quarter kilometer? You'll get to see what I'm flying through up here."

Carl spun around forward and pulled up, leaving the vicinity of the station and re-entering the traffic flow. The two Vipers were keeping a cautious pursuit, wary of Carl's free-form flying and reverse angling of his guns. He slowed to allow them to close the distance, and plowed head-on into the line of ships headed for the station. In his imagination, the two enemy pilots were swearing up a storm in their cockpits, and were probably to the point of blaming one another for their inability to finish off the lone survivor of Blue Squadron.

There was a point in the simulation coming up that was meant to test cadet reactions to unexpected turns of events. There was a corvette in the middle of the convoy that was supposed to get frustrated at the slower ships blocking its way to safe harbor. Carl angled his ship right into the impending path of the corvette, and ... he passed through as the corvette veered ... *now*. One of the two Vipers slammed into the corvette as its pilot swerved from the orderly line of fleeing ships. The trailing enemy ship flew through the debris field and right into Carl's gun sights as he spun again and hammered a full five volleys into the Viper ship before its pilot could bring its own guns to bear.

The simulator went quiet, and a humble "VICTOR" appeared on the heads-up display.

Carl tossed the reeking helm on the back of the seat and hopped out of the simulator as all the cockpit canopies opened in unison. Mriy was busily unmussing the fur around her ears. Tanny had the disapproving-but-unable-to-form-a-legitimate-complaint scowl that she'd had during most of their time as husband and wife. Adam looked up at him in awe. The Viper Squadron, across the diner, was less diverse in their opinion of Carl's flying.

"You filthy cheating ass!" one of them shouted. The three pilots storming across the establishment in the walking equivalent of squadron formation appeared to share his view. "There's no way a typhoon handles like that." He turned to the referee. "I want him disqualified."

Carl was a rich man now—at least by his personal standards. He was in a jovial mood and more than willing to rev up a hotheaded loser. "Funny, none of my wingmen think I can set a chrono by myself."

"You had a collision avoidance hack, auto-hit targeting, and I'm pretty sure decoupling the maneuvering thrusters isn't allowed in combat."

"You're just sore because you're used to picking off tourists and freighter jockeys," Carl replied. "I bet you've played dozens of battles in that thing. You learn the tricks of each simulated combat zone, and take advantage of pilots who don't know any better."

"Dozens?" the Viper leader scoffed. "Try hundreds of hours logged in these things. There's not a pilot on Delos with more flight time in a typhoon simulator."

Carl smirked. "I've never set foot in a Typhoon III simulator before today."

"Bullshit."

Tanny slid up beside him. "Are you looking to start a fight here?" she asked Carl. "If so, you can fight it yourself."

He looked to Mriy for backup. She yawned and looked away. There was always Mort, but admitting he'd brought a wizard with him was as good as admitting that he *was* a cheat. Carl held up his hands in mock surrender.

"Fine, you got me," he said. "I've never flown a Typhoon III, but I have seventy-two confirmed kills in my old Typhoon IV, plus another few thousand hours teaching advanced techniques to cadets on a Typhoon IV simulator. Only differences between it and this one here are about five percent more thruster power, an updated targeting computer, and the Naval Academy's simulators didn't smell like barbecue sauce."

"You think you're some hot shit, liar?"

"Love to stay and chat, boys, but I don't care if you believe me or not."

"Ref, who'd this guy sign in as?" the Viper leader asked.

The referee consulted his datapad. "Says here: Manfred von Richthofen."

Carl fell in with the rest of the *Mobius* crew and headed for the exit. "I'll save you the trouble. That's not my real name," he called over his shoulder.

"Ooh, you lit a fire under that rube," Roddy said. "He's gonna be bitching to all his friends on the waste reclaim freighter that he got robbed."

"Speaking of robbed, Mort, how'd we do?"

Mort cleared his throat, but said nothing.

"How much did we make?" Carl pressed. "What kind of odds did you get on us? We must have been at least ten-to-one underdogs."

Mort patted him on the shoulder. "Let it go."

Carl stopped in his tracks. The rest of the crew kept walking. "You didn't place the bet."

They stopped. "Tanny caught my eye, reminded me about our little talk."

"You know you shouldn't be gambling," Tanny said, using her wife scold. "And you were planning to bet *our* shares from the last haul?"

"It was a sure thing," said Carl.

Roddy gave him a friendly swat in the chest. "I believe in you, buddy. If it'd been up to me, I'd have let Mort bet our hard-coin on that game." He took a swig from a glass mug of Earth's Preferred that he had smuggled out of Duster's.

"Come on," said Tanny, "We've got somewhere to get. Somewhere with real money in it."

Esper gave Carl a pitying look, and he knew he was on his own. It was time to be responsible and go bring Adam home.

The *Mobius* drifted through space, on their way to the edge of the Delos system. Of course, drifting was relative. Looking out a window, there was no sense of proper scale, nothing like the blood-pumping speed of the combat simulator. In actuality, the *Mobius* was traveling a thousand times the speed of the digital Typhoons that Carl and the other pilots had flown.

Carl reclined with his feet up on the common room couch, a bacon bar in one hand, datapad in the other. Roddy and Adam were watching an animated holovid comedy, but Carl was fixated on researching Berring LX-4 transports, trying to figure out who might be interested in buying surplus escape pods. He had hardly spoken a word to Tanny since lifting off from New Melbourne and had said even less to Mort. His pockets hurt just looking at either of them.

The prospects for dealing away the escape pod were looking remote. What he found was that the Berring series was all but decommissioned due to fundamental systems flaws, a number of key systems up for recall, and a counterfeiting scam fifteen years back had flooded the market with substandard parts. Anyone who owned or operated one was more likely to be *using* the escape pods than buying replacements. It was getting damned tempting to shove Esper and Adam back in it and let someone else pick them up.

Making Adam squadron leader had been a test. Not that he expected any great strategic thinking of a ten-year-old, but for all the complexity of the subsystems, the simulator was just a fancy computer game. Kids come preprogrammed to win at those. Beating Mort at Omnithrust Racer was just proof that the kid had basic motor skills; Carl didn't even bother playing against the old wizard at anything that required quick thinking and basic tech aptitude at the same time. The fact that the races were even close called into question Adam's claims of prowess at the game. Then again, kids were stone-faced liars, the lot of them. He could respect that. It didn't make sorting the mess out any easier.

On the bright side, nothing had gone terribly wrong on Delos. Sure, his crew had murdered his hopes of scavenging three jobs' worth of cash out of one paltry haul, but that wasn't the sort of trouble he had been worrying about. If someone else had shown up to recapture Adam, Carl would have known Harmony Bay had found some way to track him, implant or no. You just couldn't trust galaxy-wide scientific syndicates not to come up with new ways of screwing people over. Maybe they had turned his DNA into an astral antenna, broadcasting his location; maybe they had a computer that could predict how his rescuers would behave; or maybe ... just maybe ... they had gotten the boy away free and clear.

Staring up through the glassed dome ceiling of the common room, he watched as Delos IX came into view. There had been no sensation of deceleration, thanks to Mort's artificial gravity being top-notch. Mort was a bastard, a backstabber, and a weasel, but he was good with gravity. Delos IX had a green atmosphere; Carl couldn't say what chemical made it that color, but it made the planet look sickly. The view was marred by the structural supports, and the presence of the manually operated dorsal turret dead center in the top. Maybe he could have Mort glass the steel supports one of these days. That bastard.

Any minute now, Mort would chase everyone out of the common room so he could plunge them into astral space. He could have done it hours ago, but on the off chance anyone was paying too close attention to the *Mobius*, Carl didn't want them to see a ship disappear from the astral sensors that watched the standard depths. As soon as they were on the far side of Delos IX, they could sneak into astral space with no one the wiser.

The ship shook, and Carl saw the flash of the ship's shields taking a hit. Dropping the datapad to the floor, he ran for the cockpit. The ship-wide comm crackled with Tanny's voice, "Mriy, take the turret. We've got incoming!"

Carl reached the cockpit at a sprint and slammed into the back of the co-pilot's seat to stop himself. "What've we got?" His eyes were already scanning the instruments.

"Hostile dropped out of astral right in front of us. Titan Nine frigate ... launched four Komodo fighters and backed off." Tanny jerked on the flight yoke, running through a basic evasive battery straight out of the marine flight manual. The ship shook with another hit.

Carl reached forward and opened a comm on an unsecured channel. "Unidentified ship ... stand down. Repeat, stand down or we will return fire."

"I just sent Mriy to return fire," Tanny said as soon as Carl closed the comm.

"Whatever. It never stops anyone from firing, but it might get them to tell us why."

"Mobius, this is the Viper. Power down your weapons and engines, and prepare to hand over the boy."

"Well, that answers that," said Carl. "Harmony Bay has it in for me personally."

"Yeah, sounds like it," Tanny agreed. The ship took another hit. "So what, hand him over or fight it out?"

"We give them Adam, and they'll just dust us anyway," said Carl. "You just slide over and let me handle the flying for this one."

"Like hell I will, after that stunt you pulled," Tanny replied, turning a shoulder to block Carl from getting past her to the flight yoke. The ship took two more hits, causing Carl to stumble. "If it weren't for you rubbing those dogs' noses in their own shit, they might not be looking to hollow us out right now." Another impact rocked them.

"Would you *stop* letting them hit us?" Carl asked.

"We have plenty of shield reserves, and Mriy needs to aim," said Tanny. "And I'm not *letting* them hit anything. Those are Komodos. They're twice as maneuverable as we are."

"Leave that to me," said Carl. "You go back there and kick Mriy off the turret controls. You're the better shot."

"Carl, just—"

"That's an order!" Carl snapped. "This is *my* ship, and I'm not ready to go down with it over a few upset stomachs."

Tanny snarled at him and slipped out of the harness. "Fine!" She shouldered past Carl and headed toward the common room and the turret. "If you get us killed, I'm coming to Hell to personally torment you," she called back.

The pilot's chair was still warm from Tanny's occupation. Sharing the warmth of a seat was about as close as they got to one another these days, but it was still comforting. As soon as Carl's hand gripped the yoke, it hit him: everyone's lives were riding on him. His palms began to sweat as he pulled them into a twisting climb. He hit the selector for the maneuvering thrusters, just as he'd done in the simulator, but nothing happened. He flipped it to the off position and back on—still nothing.

He jabbed a finger to the ship-wide comm button. "Oh, Roddy, dear," Carl singsonged through gritted teeth. "Please come up to the cockpit and *fix my goddamn ship!*"

Carl maneuvered as best he could with the computer flight assist active. They took a few more hits, with Carl juggling power to the aft shields as he kept the Komodos behind him. "*Not so smart now, tough guy?*" a voice came over the ship-to-ship comm. It was the squad leader from Duster's—possibly the sorest loser Carl had ever encountered. He felt an urge to snark back, but it was hard to come up with something clever to say when you were losing a fight.

"What's wrong?" Roddy asked, vaulting into the co-pilot's chair as soon as he entered the cockpit.

Carl's attention snapped back to the cockpit. "Manual thruster control's gone," Carl said. He saw bolts of high-energy plasma lance past the cockpit as he dodged fire.

"Yeah," said Roddy, "Safety feature at these speeds. Tanny had me upgrade it to military code."

"That's bullshit," Carl replied. "Tear out those safeties."

Roddy opened his mouth, but Carl glared plasma bolts of his own. "Sure thing, boss." The laaku stuck his head under the control console and removed a panel. Carl lost sight of him down there, but could hear the mechanic at work. He felt like a shuttle bus pilot with the way *Mobius* was handling.

"I cobble-jobbed a quick bypass," Roddy's voice echoed from inside the console. "Try now."

Carl flicked the switch for manual control, and suddenly the *Mobius* leapt at his command. He felt the rise in his stomach as the ship's movement fought against the dampening effects of

Mort's gravity enchantment and snuck some force through to the crew.

Roddy moaned from below. "I'm not going to enjoy this, am I?"

"Nope, probably not," said Carl. He was panting for breath, his heart racing. "Just head for the engine room and get ready to fix anything that breaks."

As soon as Roddy was gone, Carl squeezed his eyes shut, fighting down a wave of panic. It had been a long time since he'd flown in a live dogfight. He opened his eyes. That was it: *dogfight*. Keeping one hand on the flight yoke and twisting the ship through maneuvers by muscle memory, he opened file clusters on the *Mobius'* computer. Carl opened an archive and scanned through sub-clusters, burrowing down until he found what he was looking for.

The cluster title was "Dogfight 7" and it dated back to his navy days. He selected "play" and slid the volume indicator to maximum. In seconds, the growl of distorted guitars thundered through the cockpit. By the time the snarling vocals came in, Carl's hands had stopped shaking. He seethed out a deep breath and opened the ship-wide comm. "This is your pilot speaking. Please strap in and prepare to kick some ass. That is all."

Even with the maneuvering thrusters at his disposal, the *Mobius* was a hulking brute compared to the Komodos. It handled like the diplomatic shuttle it had been born as. In combat, it was the snapping turtle of vessels—all shell, with just enough bite to make someone wary of getting too close. Four medium-weight fighter craft were the perfect foil to use against it. Carl couldn't outrun them, and Mort couldn't take them astral while they were under fire. It was time for a new plan.

Carl dove for the planet.

Tanny's voice crackled from the turret comm. "What the hell are you doing? I can't get a track on these things with the ship jerking around, and you're going to crush us hitting atmo' at this speed."

"When was the last time they hit us?" Carl asked. "Just keep shooting. A couple lucky shots is all it'll take."

"Atmo," Tanny reiterated.

"Leave that to me."

Carl preferred to do most of his navigating by feel while under fire, but one task he always left to the computer was reentry vectors. The navigation computer blinked red with the words "No Valid Trajectory." Carl feathered back the throttle until it relented and plotted him a safe reentry angle. Just before the *Mobius* hit the atmosphere of Delos IX, Carl reached for a set of switches he had hardly ever needed. The shields were washed in flame as the gasses that swirled around the planet ignited, setting off beeping alarms that temporarily interrupted the music blaring through the cockpit.

He hit the switches, and the shields reshaped. Instead of an egg-shaped blob around the ship, they stretched, sharpened, and took on an aerodynamic profile, tied into the flight yoke. Roddy had given him a barrel of grief over installing it, but Carl had wanted it for just this sort of emergency. The *Mobius* bled speed as it forced its way through the clouds of the uninhabited world. The beeping alarms stopped as the ship's momentum was no longer enough to burn the atmosphere around them, and the next song came on. This time it was a heavy instrumental piece with a hammering bass line and primitive synthesizer.

On the radar, the four Komodo ships were slowing down and entering the atmosphere well behind him. *Mobius's* shields were sturdy enough to allow them to come in with more speed without burning up. Carl continued his dive, watching through the murky green haze for signs of terrain. He pulled up when he saw a mountain range, which might have been eerily beautiful had he stopped to enjoy it. Rocky spires shot into the emerald heavens, larger than the greatest peaks of Earth or Mars.

He keyed the comm to the turret. "I'll try to string 'em out through the mountains. Atmosphere should slow them down more than us."

"How much of our shield power did you just throw away?" Tanny asked.

Carl shrugged, even though he knew she couldn't see him. "Some. Just keep those guns warm."

He banked as he pulled the *Mobius* through a valley between two enormous peaks. He saw flashes of plasma slam into the mountainsides to the starboard side of the ship. The Komodos were behind him and trying to close in, thrusters plowing their semi-aerodynamic hulls through the atmosphere. The *Mobius* took three hits in rapid succession; Carl crested one peak and dove down one behind them.

One of the Komodos disappeared from radar. "Got one," Tanny shouted over the comm. Another shot hit the shields, causing the aerodynamic shape to fluctuate. A momentary panic came over Carl as the ship lurched toward the ground, but the shields reformed and he was able to pull up.

Another blip vanished from the radar. Carl opened the ship-to-ship. "Not so fancy now, huh, you burger-hustling sim-jockeys? Stick to the restaurant circuit; the ocean's too deep for you boys."

The last two fighters broke off pursuit, but Carl was past the bygones point. There came a time in any battle when letting the other guy go just sat wrong in a pilot's stomach—when the fight got too personal, the ramifications too complicated to think of in the heat of the moment. Maybe the other guy would never want to think about the incident again; maybe it would turn into a vendetta. With those angry red blips still flashing in the radar screen, the solution seemed obvious. Caution demanded fiery wreckage, and mercy seemed like a fool's plan.

Carl pulled up, rolled, and twisted the *Mobius* around to give chase. The cockpit shuddered as the shields took the brunt of the high G-force maneuvering, straining the generators to maintain the shields' shape. Ignoring the warning lights of impending shield overload, Carl hammered the throttle open, blood still pumping in time with the rhythm of the bass. For once, he took Tanny's need to aim into account and held a steady course, taking a gentle hand to the yoke as he kept on the tails of the two remaining Komodos.

Carl clucked his tongue. "Not even splitting up?" he muttered, not even able to hear his own voice. He was tempted to open fire with the *Mobius's* forward guns, but he could see Tanny's shots tracking them, now that the battle was taking place in front of him. She had everything under control. First one, then the other Komodo burst into a cloud of shrapnel and plume of ignited oxygen.

Carl shut down the music and let out a whoop. When he caught his breath, he keyed the ship-wide comm. "All clear everyone. Roddy, run a quick check, make sure we're not leaking anything important. Mort, get ready to drop us astral as soon as I bring us back to our departure point."

He climbed out of the atmosphere, disengaging the aerodynamic shielding effect. As he did so, he took his first close look at the shield status readout: five percent. It was closer than he had meant to cut things, but the engines seemed intact, and they would power back up while the *Mobius* traveled between systems.

"Carl!" Tanny shouted over the comm. "You forgot the carrier!"

His eyes first widened, then shot over to the radar. Around the far side of the planet came the *Viper* on an intercept course. The *Mobius* was only a third of the *Viper's* displacement, and outgunned, but they had speed on their side. Carl fired the maneuvering thrusters and swung them full about, aiming out to the deep ocean between stars. The safety harness bit into his shoulder as the inertia tried to throw him across the cockpit despite the ship's gravity spell. Once more, Carl opened up the throttle to full, thinking to get far enough ahead that they could escape astrally. Even if the *Viper* had scanners that could sweep between standard astral depths, he doubted they could go deep enough to keep up. The *Mobius* would just need to—

The ship shook, and Carl's neck whipped forward. Spots swam before his eyes. When he blinked his vision back to working order, they were adrift. The shield indicator read zero. Main thrusters had gone out. The *Viper* hailed them.

"Mobius, stand down and prepare to be boarded. Resistance will be met with deadly force. Turn the boy over unharmed, or you're all as good as dead."

The floor bucked under Carl's feet as he ran for his quarters. The *Viper* had latched on with capture claws. "They're coming for us!" he shouted on the way. Realizing that not everyone could hear him, he hit the common room ship-wide comm. "Arm yourselves and prepare to repel boarders."

In his quarters, he dug through the hastily stored weapons that had been unearthed as if from an ancient tomb during the Tally-ho's inspection. He belted on a holster with the blaster already in. He drew the weapon, popped the power pack out, checked that it was full, and snapped it back into the grip. Three more power packs slipped into his pockets. Turning to leave, he had a stray thought and returned for his runed graphite sword. If the power packs ran out, he didn't want to go unarmed.

A klaxon blared, letting everyone aboard know that there was a hull breach. Carl was only marginally worried about losing pressure. They wanted Adam alive, and that meant cutting through the hull someplace where the *Viper's* people had life support latched onto the far side. He brushed aside the idea of grabbing his EV helmet and rushed to the cargo hold.

He got as far as the doorway.

The *Viper* had cut through the cargo bay door near the center, and invaders were firing up at the walkway, where Mriy and Tanny were already armed and returning fire. The corner of the common room by the refrigerator had become their bunker. Carl ducked as splats of low-energy plasma whizzed through the open door. He bent in half as he slunk up beside Tanny to get a status.

"How's it looking?" he asked.

Tanny was armed with a blaster rifle, and was poking it around with a blind scope to lay down suppression fire. "Oh, just peachy. Ship that size, they've probably got us outnumbered four to one. The only grace we've gotten is that they're trying not to vent the ship to space; otherwise, they'd have shot right through the walls."

"I cannot reach them," Mriy said. "Perhaps we let them advance?"

"That's the backup plan," Tanny replied. "For now we keep firing and hope we hit a few. They're here for the money; they might not like their payout if they see a few buddies die."

Carl tried to think as the klaxon blared, but all he could come up with was to join Tanny and Mriy in firing back at the boarders. Standing above Tanny's crouch, he reached his blaster around and squeezed off three shots. He pulled his hand back before someone took a shot and blew it off.

Tanny checked in her scope. "You barely hit the wall they breached."

"Where's Roddy?" Carl asked. "Maybe he can rig up something to power those disintegrator rifles from the power packs we've got."

"The rifles are halfway between us and them," Tanny said. "We can't even *get* to them. I sent Roddy down to see if he can get us engine power for a breakaway."

"Good idea," Carl said, nodding.

Plasma bolts continued to come intermittently, the invaders conserving their power, trying to time a shot as someone poked a weapon at them. They had nothing but time on their hands, as far as they knew. Carl snapped a few shots around the doorway, then winced as a bolt of plasma caught his blaster. Composite plastic shards sprayed from the shattered weapon. He clapped a hand to the side of his neck where it felt like a bee had stung him.

"Carl!" Tanny shouted. "You're hit."

He gritted his teeth as he put his back to the wall and slid down to a seated position. "I noticed that."

"Shit, you're bleeding," Tanny said. She turned toward the crew quarters, just a few meters away. "Esper, get out here and help him; he's cut bad."

Mriy's ears flattened against her head, and she hunkered back against the side of the refrigerator. "Death comes."

"Come on," said Carl. "Let's not write me off just yet." Mriy shook her head and pointed.

There was a thump of wood on steel, and then another, a drumbeat of calm menace playing counterpoint to the frantic shriek of the klaxon. They turned and saw what Mriy had seen. Mort emerged from his quarters clad in black robes, a chain of heavy silver links around his neck, bearing a graven pendant. The thumping was the staff he carried as a walking stick. His scowl carried the weight of storms; his eyes promised fire. With casual disdain he slammed the head of his staff against the wall, and the klaxon stopped.

"Mort," Carl grunted as he tried to hold back the flow of blood from his neck. "What are you doing?"

"Mort, no!" Tanny warned. "We've talked about this. We need the ship's tech to stay alive."

"Mordecai The Brown will not meet his end cowering behind the paltry protections of science. If this is to be our end, let there be a reckoning in blood and fire. I'm going to show these fuckers something very, very old."

He strode past the three defenders at the door. None tried to bar his path as he presented himself in full glory before the open door. He leveled his staff at the invaders that only his vantage allowed him to see, and cursed in that harsh, guttural language that spoke of demons and angels. From the staff came fire, and the lights in the common room went dark. By the time the soft, red emergency lighting came on, Mort was gone, disappeared down into the cargo hold, and perhaps beyond, to do battle with the crew of the *Viper*.

The door to Chip's old quarters opened. "Stay put," Esper said, speaking back inside as she peeked out. "What's going on out here?"

"Carl took a piece of shrapnel to his neck," Tanny replied. "Go find the med kit."

Esper closed the door behind her and hurried to Carl's side. She saw the blood seeping from between his fingers where they covered his neck. Kneeling down beside him, she turned to Tanny. "I don't know where it is. You go; I'll stay with him."

"I need to cover the—"

"I heard Mort's little speech. And I don't hear any more shooting. Just go."

Tanny glared at Esper, but didn't argue the point. Carl managed a weak smile as she left. "She hates getting the fun taken out of her hand ... I mean gun."

"Just you relax," Esper said. "Now take your hand away." To

reinforce her point, she tugged gently at the hand that was staunching the blood. Instantly it spurted forth, but she covered the wound with her hands. Carl grimaced, and grunted in pain as she pressed down.

Through squinted eyes, Carl saw her lips moving. She had her eyes closed. In the dim crimson light, she looked unhallowed, like someone had come and replaced Sister Esper Theresa Richelieu with a creature of magic and darkness, performing a foul ritual. For a moment, Carl thought it was his imagination, exacerbated by blood loss. Then a stabbing pain clenched at his stomach and latched on. He doubled over in pain, and Esper let go of his neck.

"Get him something from the fridge," Esper ordered Mriy. The azrin looked at her with narrowed eyes, uncomprehending. "He needs food; his body just used up its reserves healing itself."

"Gah," Carl grunted. "What'd you *do* to me?"

"I sinned, but I may have saved your life," Esper replied.

The crackle of flames and a whiff of brimstone in the air hearkened back to the battlefields of Mort's ancestors. Too often he felt bottled up, squeezed into a tin can in the vast Black Ocean, unable to unleash his magic for fear of fouling the bedratted technology that kept them afloat. Putting on his formal Convocation robes had seemed like vanity at first, but as fire leapt from his staff and his voice boomed thunder, the old confidence returned. A pained groan from the floor told him that one of his would-be killers was still alive. Mort jabbed the butt of his staff down at the half-burnt pirate; the wood tip never touched the man, but the deck plates beneath buckled at the force of an unseen blow. He left the corpse in a shallow depression newly formed in the floor.

He stumbled. One footstep was too light as the ship's gravity wavered for a moment, then reverted to normal. Mort's eyes narrowed. Someone was fiddling with the ship's gravity stone, and he had a fair guess of who it might be. A ship the *Viper's* size ought to have had its own mechanics aboard for both scientific and magical devices. The poor slob of a science mechanic could have been any of a number of corpses littering the ship, but he had yet to run across anything resembling a wizard.

In theory, Mort knew precisely where he was heading—the ship's gravity stone, nestled somewhere below him and roughly fifty feet to his right. The problem was that the ship was made by engineers. The layout was nonsense. Mort spent the better part of five minutes punching buttons on a door-side control panel to no avail. After melting a hole through the door made from a not-quite-metal scientific material, all he found beyond was a lavatory.

"What bumbling nutter locks a loo from the outside?" he muttered.

Three melted door-holes later, the found the stairs down to the lower level. The air was growing foul with acrid smoke from dead bodies and the strange substance the doors were fashioned from. Despite the stale, processed smell below, it was easier to breathe as he went down. Fortunately, once he was on the same level as the gravity stone, it was easier to find his way. One door opened at his approach, startling Mort, and one more yielded to magical coercion.

The room inside was thick with science, but arcane energy thrummed beneath. At the far wall was a set of crystal and stone rods held together in a lattice of wires—the *Viper's* star drive. In the center of the room, set atop a scientific steel pedestal, was a sphere of pure, Earth-quarried granite—a gravity stone. It was not the decorative, mineral-veined granite found in bar-tops and decorative flooring, but the plain, serious sort used in ancient headstones. Standing between these two wonders of modern magic was a sniveling excuse for a wizard.

"Stay back," the *Viper's* star drive mechanic warned, his hands resting on the gravity stone. "I can crush you where you stand."

Mort felt a twinge. *You are heavy*, the universe told him. *You are being crushed into a tiny ball centered just behind your navel.* The sensation was that of a giant mitten closing around him— soft, smothering, and firm. It was a sign that this pissant wretch of a grav-jockey was adept at his business—Mort was surprised to feel anything at all.

Like hell I am, Mort replied to the universe, asserting his own self-image through an act of will. *Quit bothering me if you know what's good for you.* He had never shied from threats made by the greater universe around him, and was not about to stand idly by while it tried to convince him he was a source of gravity.

Mort jabbed a bony finger down on the surface of the gravity stone. The granite split in twain with the crack of a sledgehammer's strike. "Care to try that again?" he asked with a smile of feigned sweetness.

"Wh-who are you?" the star drive mechanic asked, backing away from the ruined stone. Though the *Viper's* gravity still functioned, it was bleeding away and in no shape to be used as a weapon. When Mort took a step forward instead of answering, his staff thumping on the deck like a funeral bell, the mechanic threw up his hands in surrender. "I'll serve; two years indentured. You've got me." Mort took another step. "It's bad luck to kill a wizard."

"That's because the Convocation used to send wizards like me after the ones who killed them," Mort relied. "I am Mordecai The Brown, former holder of the Eighth Seat, Guardian of the Plundered Tomes, and current *persona non grata* with the higher-ups in the Convocation, so I'm not registering any apprentices.

But if you mention my name in the afterlife, I'm sure there's a support group for wizards I've killed."

The star drive mechanic gave a choked gasp. Without the *Viper's* gravity stone objecting, it was a simple matter to convince the universe that it was the mechanic whose body was the wellspring of gravity aboard. The mechanic crumpled into the fetal position in mid-air, while a datapad and the contents of a toolbox leapt to press against him. Mort didn't drag things out; this wasn't personal, after all. He squeezed, and the lights went out in the ship. A few crackles and pops, and he allowed the mechanic's body to flop to the floor with a wet splat. "*Kirash,*" he whispered, and the end of his staff glowed with enough light to see the mass of twisted and broken limbs at his feet.

Mort coughed. The air was getting worse. The whoosh and hum that was the undercurrent of any ship's environmental controls had gone silent. It was not the sort of thing Mort typically took note of, but its absence shouted alarm to him. Stumbling through a haze of magically illuminated smoky corridors, he made his way back to the *Mobius* before he passed out.

In the wake of most battles, the smoke cleared. When Mort stumbled back into the common room, coughing and batting the smoke from his robes, there was no functioning life support system to disperse it. Carl slammed the common room door closed behind the wizard. Everyone who had EV suits had already changed into them. Tanny, Mriy, and Carl were waiting in the common room for Mort to return, while Roddy was down in the engineering bay, trying to see what he could patch back together. Esper, Adam, and now Mort were all without environmental protection.

"Boss," Roddy came over the comm in Carl's helm. "We got a

whole lot of nothing. Good news: nothing looks beyond repair. Bad news: this isn't gonna be quick."

"You've got to come up with something for the life support," Carl replied. "We're short three EV suits for a long-term plan. Even the life support in the crew quarters aren't—"

"I'm the one who told you, remember?"

"Just ... go fix something," Carl replied. "Life support first ... salvage stuff from the *Viper* if you need to."

"It safe over there?" Roddy asked.

Carl relayed the question to the wizard. "How would I know?" Mort replied. "Starships are inherently *un*safe. I tell you this much, there's no one over there in enough pieces to point a weapon at you."

"Yeah, Roddy. It's all clear."

"Wait," said Tanny. "What if we stashed them in that damned albatross of an escape pod you can't get rid of?"

It was hard to give a withering look through the smoky plastic visor of an EV helmet, but Carl gave his best effort anyway. "After all Mort just did ... you can't tell me that piece of junk took all that?"

"Do lights and blinky things mean it was working?" asked Mort. It was an astounding observation on his part, on par with the time he managed to use the ship-wide comm. "Because it had things blinking."

"Let's get Adam and Esper something to cover their faces to make a run for it," said Carl.

"... and speaking of things not working," Mort continued. "I thought you were bleeding out your last drops just a few minutes ago."

"Ask Esper about it," Carl said. "You three might be cooped up in there a while."

"Me?" Mort scoffed. "But I don't—"

"I offered you an EV suit years ago, and you didn't want one. Time to live with that decision. Now get moving; air's a wasting."

The door swung shut and latched with a quick hiss of compressed air. They were sealed in. Mort slumped down into one of the four seats in the escape pod with a huff, folding his arms. He brought with him more of the smoky smell that had only started to dissipate as the pod's life support system worked to filter the air. He harrumphed.

"Looks like we're stuck here a while," said Mort.

Esper nodded. She couldn't think of anything she wanted to say to the wizard. She kept as far from him as the tight confines of the escape pod allowed.

"How comes this thing still works?" Adam asked. "Just about everything else broke."

Mort scowled. "How should I know? Far as I can tell, most of this stuff shouldn't work in the first place. It's all plastic and wires and whatnot with tiny sparks of lightning chasing each other around inside. But then, that's science at work for you; never makes a lick of proper sense."

"Don't you go filling the boy's head with nonsense," said Esper. "Science works, and if you took the time to study it, you'd see how, too."

Mort waved a hand in her direction and looked away. "I've heard it all before. The professors, the researchers, the would-be science evangelists. They pull out Newton and Einstein and Hawking, and tell me those tidy little equations make it all work. I counter with del Braham, Miang, and Copperfield. It all goes round in circles 'til everyone's hackles are up and no one's convinced anyone of anything."

"But science works," Adam said. "I mean, there's proof."

Mort shrugged. "Never said it didn't. Just not my preferred modus."

"No, you prefer blasting things with fire," Esper snapped.

Mort chuckled. "Is *that* what has your snoot in a snit? I figured a science fanatic would approve. I took a big problem and reduced it to smaller pieces."

"I'm not a science fanatic," Esper protested. "But misusing God's power is a sin."

"I used my own power. God's got plenty of His own," said Mort. "And like hell I sinned. I saved all of us. From what I've gathered, *you* have a bit of your own."

Esper swallowed. She had hoped to avoid this conversation. "I learned that trick a long time ago, before I heard the calling. Even for good cause, it was a sin, and I'll do penance for it."

"Long time ago? A long time ago your parents hadn't met. You haven't got a long time in you, period," said Mort. "You saved Carl's life, and you're ready to throw yourself up on a cross for it. I killed nineteen people just a few minutes ago, and I'm feeling pretty damned heroic, if I must say. Which one of us has his priorities straight?"

"*Their* priorities," Adam said.

"Huh?"

"You presupposed an answer with the masculine pronoun," Adam replied. "It's a nasty trick. You asked a question with just one answer."

"He didn't mean to—" Esper said, but Mort cut her off with a laugh.

"Guilty, I admit. We could make a wizard out of you yet, boy."

Adam frowned, but that just caused Mort to laugh anew.

"So how's a sweet, spoiled thing like you learn a bit of magic, anyway?" Mort asked. "Your parents have retrogressive views on education, or something?"

"I'd rather not talk about it."

"Suit yourself," Mort replied. "But we've got nothing to do but wait out the repairs, and if Carl's in a helpful mood, it might be a while. If you ignore the boy, you could even consider it confession. Not like you're going to find a more sympathetic soul when it comes to magic."

"Confession isn't about sympathy; it's about compassion and understanding the temptation of sin, and the cleansing of the soul afterward."

"There are only seven real sins, you know," Mort said. "Convince me which you broke, and I'll admit you sinned in saving Carl."

Esper remained quiet. He was baiting her. Wizards were devilishly clever by training and by nature, and Mort wouldn't have asked if he wasn't prepared to counter her answers.

Mort leaned forward. "Did you know that Earth is the only world to hear God's word and think he meant for us not to use magic? The Seekers have shown it's all the same religion, all the same root, and yet Earth is the only place where you're a heretic for practicing the ancient ways. Among Mriy's people, you'd be revered. Roddy's would consider you duty-bound to use that power of yours to help people."

"I've never met a Seeker," Esper replied, hanging her head. "I was raised in the One Church. We didn't consort with those sorts."

"You should," said Mort. "Otherwise, you're doomed to self-loathing and self-flagellation for doing what your heart tells you is right. A man who tells you he has all the answers is lying to himself and to you. A man who admits he knows nothing is a man you should turn to for advice. Whoever taught you that trick of magic was a proper saint."

Esper snorted. "I never thought I'd hear anyone call Tamra Dawson a saint."

Mort raised an eyebrow, and Esper sighed. "We were just kids, really," she said. "I was fourteen, maybe fifteen at the time. I'd just gotten these." She bared her perfect white teeth in neither a smile nor a snarl. "Mine weren't straight, and even if they got straightened, they weren't shaped just right. My mother had them replaced with ceramite implants. They only let me use painkillers the first few days, but the pain lasted weeks. Tamra's parents were the same way with her; she'd gone in for more upgrades and adjustments than I ever had. She'd picked up this trick, you see—never told me where. It speeds up your body's own healing. I didn't even realize it was magic at first; I just thought it was one of those hokey ancient get-well-by-thinking-well mantras. But it worked. I got good at it. I'd come back from the cosmo half patched up—natural healing's supposed to make the results look smoother. Next day, I'd be fine, but I'd eat my way through a week's meals."

Mort nodded. "I wouldn't mind learning a trick like that. Sounds damned handy."

"I practiced. I got good at it. I needed to, since my mother was never satisfied. Teeth, irises, ears, cheekbones. I've had my nose reshaped three times because she changed her mind about what looked best on me. Breasts, hips, buttocks, feet, fingers, and ribs, all adjusted to her liking. It took six tries shaping my vocal chords and soft palette until she liked my voice. Every follicle on my body has been replaced or removed. But it was when she decided to take me in for personality softening that I ran."

Mort reached across the pod and put a hand on her shoulder. She flinched, but his touch was gentle and warm. "And you did the right thing."

"My body barely has any fat cells left," she said, sniffing. "I can't go long periods without eating because my body can't store it."

"I meant with Carl," Mort said. "But running away was right, too. Everyone here's running from something. It's the sort of place for people who don't belong."

"Chocolate bar?" Adam asked. Producing one from his pocket. Leave it to a ten-year-old to take provisions for sequestration of unknown duration and pack candy.

"Yes, thank you." Esper snatched the bar, perhaps too violently to be considered polite, and tore the wrapper off. She bit into the bar and savored not just the flavor, but the gritty texture of the chocolate. "Where'd you get this?" she asked after swallowing her first bite.

"They're Tanny's, I think," Mort said. Esper stopped cold. There was no feasible way to un-eat a bite of chocolate and put the wrapper back around it, but if there were she would have done it in an instant.

Mort just laughed. "Don't worry. I won't tell her. For all she'll know, Adam ate it. I'm a fair hand at keeping secrets. For instance, I haven't mentioned to anyone about that pendant you wear ... and I don't mean your order's cross."

Esper felt her face warm. There was no way he could know. Or could he? He was a wizard after all. "It's just sentimental. I've had it forever."

"Forever, or since you were ... oh, eleven, maybe twelve or thirteen? Helps you out once a month, give or take? I can sniff out an enchantment as easily as you smell chocolate in the air. But like I said, I can keep a secret. I imagine you must be able to, too. The One Church is rather particular on that subject."

Esper offered a weak smile. "None of them noticed, so I never said anything. It's not against the vows."

"What vows?" Adam asked.

Mort cleared his throat. "So, how long you think those repairs are going to take?"

Carl wished he had sent Tanny over to the *Viper*. She had the stronger stomach. Other navy officers, active and retired alike, kept up a stubborn rivalry with the marines, but Carl would never begrudge them the ability to walk through a pile of bodies without getting sick. There was no unseeing the things that Mort had done to the crew of the hostile vessel. All he could say for the wizard's work was that it didn't look like any of the mercenaries suffered long, and that with a strong enough alkaline solution, most of it would clean up. But Tanny was helping Roddy get the *Mobius* spaceworthy again, and Carl's errand was less than vital in that regard. In the near term thereafter, what he was looking for could be crucial.

The *Viper* was roomier than the *Mobius*, the interior all colored in garish spray-art; probably the work of one of the crew. It was hard to imagine any captain *paying* to have that sort of thing done to virtually every interior surface of his ship, but then again, some captains had strange tastes. The haze of smoke made the air murky and caught the light from Carl's hand lamp. There was no emergency lighting on board, but here and there an indicator blinked, showing that there was power at work somewhere to supply it. It was as good a sign as Carl could hope for. He headed toward the cockpit.

It was strange at times, being a fighter pilot by trade. His destination was, by all standard parlance, a bridge. Yet any enclosed space dedicated to flying made him revert to Typhoon jargon. The *Viper's* bridge was abandoned. It appeared as if all hands had been called to battle Mort. Aside from the haze of smoke and the lack of ambient light, it looked serviceable. He sat down in the captain's chair and hit a button at random on the armrest console. It lit.

"Hey Roddy," he called over the comm. "How's things?"

"You know," the comm crackled, "This really isn't the time to be riding my ass. Just leave me the hell alone to do my job. When the ship's fixed, you'll be the first to know."

"Sorry, just thought you might be interested to hear that the *Viper* has power to her bridge."

"You gotta be fucking kidding me," Roddy replied. "Mort fried the *Mobius* worse than their scrap heap? I installed all that obsidian for nothing?"

"We planned ahead for gravity and astral drive," Carl replied. "We didn't have a contingency for Mort impersonating Genghis Khan."

"I'm going to have to tell Mort that one," said Tanny. It was an open comm among the EV helms and the cockpit, so Tanny and Mriy heard everything they said. "He'd get a kick."

"Who is Genkis Khan?" Mriy asked.

"Human from about a million years ago," Carl replied. He didn't know exactly, and Mriy probably didn't care. "He killed half a continent's worth of people using tech like the azrins had before the rest of the galaxy discovered you."

"I think I like him," Mriy replied.

"So how 'bout it Roddy?" Carl asked. "With the two ships joined up, could we use the *Viper's* life support to clear both ships?"

"You owe me a beer," Roddy replied.

"I what?"

"Not you," Tanny replied. "I bet him you'd be more trouble than help."

"Thanks."

"Anytime."

Carl settled back in the captain's chair and fiddled with the controls until he got the main screen to display the communications logs. It was reverse chronological and had both voice transcriptions and text communiques intermixed. It was fancy. If Carl wanted to keep records of his comm traffic, he had to link a datapad to the *Mobius's* computer. After skipping past the conversation between himself and the *Viper's* captain—which carried a strange sense of deja vu—he found what he was looking for:

0832:05:15:2560   C.B.DYSON: 75000 NOW, REST WHEN ADAM DELIVERED SAFELY.

DESTINATION TBD. ADAM WILL INFORM YOU AFTER RETRIEVAL. TRANSMITTING COURSE DATA.

"Gotcha."

"What's that?" Tanny asked. Carl had spoken with the comm still open. It was damnably inconvenient to turn off and on while wearing the helmet.

"You three, change of plans. Get over to the *Viper's* cockpit. I need you all to see something."

The hours passed, and the inside of the escape pod grew ever smaller. The walls stayed where they were of course; it was Esper's need to be on the other side of them that kept growing. She kept looking out into the cargo bay through the pod's tiny windows, looking for a glimpse of one of the crew in their EV suits or for some sign that the smoke was clearing. The problem was that the lights were so low outside the pod that the glare from the ones inside kept her from seeing much. To his credit, Mort had kept up a lively conversation to drag her mind away from their predicament.

"... and that's when I knew that we were going to be stuck with Mriy on board," Mort said, finishing what must have been his twentieth anecdote.

"So it was all a misunderstanding?" Adam asked. "She didn't mean to kill him?"

Mort twisted his face and scratched his chin with one finger.

"I can't say for certain. Oh, I'm sure she didn't start out meaning to kill her brother. Her kind fights for dominance in the family as a matter of course. It's just ... well, there are rules for that sort of thing, she didn't follow them, and it happened. Azrin don't think much is wrong with killing in general, but within the family they don't put up with it."

"Hopefully, the longer they're exposed to human—I mean civilized—cultures, the more they'll respect life," Esper said. "Mriy doesn't seem as bad as I've heard her kind are, but she's still a savage."

"No one's as bad as the stories about their people," Mort countered. "You should hear the stories they tell about us, especially in regards to dark science. I mean, just look at the two of us; then, consider those bastards who mucked up Adam's brain, not to mention cloning him."

Adam frowned. "My brain's not mucked up. The doctors even said so."

"Well, now there's a—"

A thump from the door ended the debate abruptly. With a hiss of equalizing pressure, Esper's ears popped and the door opened. Carl stood outside, still in his EV suit. He pressed a helmet into her hands, and tossed another to Mort. "Put those on and come out here. Adam, stay put."

"What's this all about?" Mort asked.

"We're wasting the pod's air. I'll explain outside."

Esper put hers on with some trepidation. The helmet had to have come from the *Viper*. She could only pray that it had not been taken from the dead. The rubber membrane sealed against the underside of her chin, and she took a deep breath. It was stale air, but the purified, sterile sort of stale, and there was no smell of anything unsavory having happened inside it recently.

Mort glared at Carl from beneath one raised eyebrow, but crammed the helmet over his head. "I feel like an idiot."

"You look like one," Carl said. "Now, get out so we don't let Adam's air out."

Mriy was standing by to close the pod door and seal Adam safely back inside.

"So, what's this all about?" Mort asked. "Why am I dressed up like some medieval motorcycle knight?"

"Sister Theresa, I think you have a holy duty to see to," Carl said. "We're about to inter nineteen men and women on Delos IX, and that ship is their coffin. We've cleared the ship; it's safe. Go do what you need to do."

Esper nodded. She found herself wondering whether it was pious to be thankful for such a grim duty. Alone among heathens and heretics, she was being asked to be a priestess once more.

"What about me?" Mort asked. "What am I out here for?"

"As soon as she's done, you're going to turn that place into a pyre."

Esper walked away down the boarding tunnel and into the *Viper*. It was a scene she was never going to forget. She had seen death before, but it was the whispering sort: age, disease, or more commonly a combination of both. This was death that howled. Bodies burnt like candle wicks lay shoved against the walls. Others had been torn to pieces by forces she could not imagine, drenching whole corridors in splattered blood, through which trails of footprints tracked in both directions. There was little doubt that the *Viper's* crew died in poor standing with the Lord. There were no mortally wounded to be brought back into grace before the end. It was all she could do to intercede on their behalf in death.

She wept, and prayed, and hoped fervently not to be sick inside her borrowed EV helmet.

"Fine," said Mort, "Now that she's out of earshot, can you tell me what's going on? Like hell you want me using more magic in that ship."

"Of course not," Carl replied, pulling off his EV helmet. He pointed a finger to Roddy, who flicked on a plasma torch and tack welded the door to the escape pod shut.

Mort scowled, but Carl could see the water-wheels turning the wizard's brain. "You got me. What's the punchline?"

Carl handed Mort a datapad with a transcription of the *Viper's* log. Mort took it gingerly by the edges and squinted down at it. After a moment, he straightened. Balancing the datapad in one hand like a serving platter, he tore the helmet from his head and threw it at Carl. "Air's fine out here."

"Yeah, Roddy got life support back up a couple hours ago. We needed you to see this first, before Esper."

Mort scanned the datapad for a moment. "This doesn't make any sense. C.B. Dyson is Chip, I presume. But why would Chip sell us out? How would he even have known about Adam? Was Chip in on this from the start?"

"Look at the date," Carl prodded.

Mort squinted and held the datapad closer. "What on this infernal thing is supposed to be a date?"

Carl grabbed the datapad out of the wizard's hands and pointed. "Right there. Those numbers, that's a date. Today's date."

Mort's eyes widened in dawning comprehension. "Chip's still alive! Or back from the dead. Either way, he seems hell-bound on avenging himself on Adam, whom he probably blames for his—"

"Mort, it's not Chip, it's someone using Chip's ID," Carl replied. "This message was sent from the *Mobius* after we set course out of Delos. Using Chip's rig. From his quarters."

"From his quarters ..." Mort repeated. "Not Esper!"

"No," Carl replied. "Adam."

"Why would the boy kidnap himself?"

Carl led Mort by the arm away from the escape pod. There was no way Adam should have been able to hear from inside, but he was beyond the point of taking those sorts of risks. "He's not. He's buying himself free. Esper's plan to rescue him is naive; it's going to get him picked up by Harmony Bay again. He wants a clean break, to disappear, all witnesses disposed of."

"That means us," Roddy clarified as he walked over to join them.

"How? Where would the boy get that kind of money?" Mort asked.

"Doctor James Augustus Cliffton," Carl said with a smug smile.

Mort shook a finger in Carl's direction. "Now, wait just a minute. Esper said that dark scientist was dead. We had a long talk in that infernal pod, and she mentioned checking up on him while she waited on Adam's tests at the hospital. Was that a trick, or is this some elaborate scam?"

"The most elaborate scam I can think of. I'm convinced that Adam *is* Doctor Cliffton."

"But that's ... now wait just a minute ... you're saying that little boy is a one-hundred twelve-year-old man?" Mort asked.

Carl nodded. "It explains everything. Adam's tried ditching us at Willamette Station, but we 'rescued' him. He saw some unsavories at Duster's who looked like they might be for hire and had a grudge, and transmitted our coordinates and heading. I bet he even arranged for that escape pod to jam in the first place; he's been trying to lose Esper since before he met us. Who knows what else he tried that we never saw; all the records on our end are encrypted or destroyed. Doctor Cliffton *is* an expert with Chip's stuff. I had to dig into the *Viper's* computers to find proof."

"And he put the Tally-ho on our trail, too, I bet," Mort said.

"Maybe, but I'm guessing it was just Penny-Toad doing his

job, policing the smuggling lanes. Getting picked up by a Navy patrol wouldn't do him much good."

"So what now?" Mort asked. "We toss him out a window in that pod?"

Carl chuckled. "It's tempting, but no. I've got something better in mind. But first I needed to know I had you on board. Now? Now, I've got the hard part."

It was as embarrassing as it was sad, losing count of the dead. Esper could have convinced herself of anywhere from seventeen to twenty. She was no forensics expert to say whose remains were whose, and where one began and another ended. The few who died alone were easiest. The filter on the EV helm kept away the smell and put a barrier of translucent plastic between her eyes and the horrors around her. It was all that kept her from being sick at the sights around her. Through the visor, she could imagine that it was all just a vivid simulation. A vague worry gnawed at her that she wasn't praying for real men and women, but for mere holograms.

The footsteps startled her into a gasp. Could there have been a survivor? As it turned out, it was just Carl in an EV helmet. The nonchalant swagger that he took wherever he went was absent. She almost wished he had been flippant about the carnage, just so she could chastise him for his part in it. Mort had been so ... proud wasn't the right word ... righteous, perhaps? It had been hard to argue with him. After all, she was only alive because of his intervention; so were the rest of them. Barring a miracle, the crew of the *Viper* would have killed them, and demanding a miracle was the epitome of Pride.

"You good here?" Carl asked, sweeping a pointed finger around the floor.

"No," she snapped, finding the opening she needed to vent her frustration. "There's nothing good here at all. Vile men or not, these deaths are on your hands, and you should treat them with a little more—"

"Easy; easy. I'm sorry," Carl said, holding up his hands. "But it's not me who brewed this batch of vinegar. Wasn't Mort either; he just cleaned it up ... well, clean maybe isn't the right word. But come up to the bridge and I'll show you who's to blame."

"Who?" she asked.

"I need you to see this for yourself," Carl replied. "I seem to recall bragging about being a lying sonofabitch, so I think the *Viper's* computers have a bit more credibility."

Esper followed Carl toward the front of the ship. "And you couldn't have altered this ship's records?"

Carl looked over his shoulder as he walked, the EV helmet masking his expression behind six millimeters of smoky black plastic. "You've been bunking in our computer guy's quarters; you performed his funeral yourself. Maybe it's your turn to show a little respect. These sim-hustlers were trying to kill us; Chip was family."

Esper followed quietly after that. It was true, everyone in the crew knew Carl was a gifted liar; they seemed oddly proud of it. But there was something in his voice that she had to believe was genuine—unless that was just how good a liar he truly was. At some point, she had to trust to her own judgment and decide whether he was the man he claimed to be, lies and all.

When the cockpit door closed behind her, Carl took off his helmet. "Air's clean enough to breathe. Just didn't want to smell Mort's handiwork." He pointed to the captain's chair. "Have a seat."

Esper obliged and set her own EV helmet at her feet. "What am I looking at?"

"Pull up the ship's comm log, starting with today and working backward."

"What am I looking for in there?"

"It stands out a bit. Don't worry."

The armrest console was simple enough to operate that she had no trouble with the unfamiliar system. For a mercenary vessel, the buttons and screens were all bright, cheerful, and helpful. In moments she had brought up the most recent communications to and from the *Viper*. She read the past day's entries with particular attention to detail as a hollow feeling welled inside her. Hoping she had missed some crucial detail, she read them once more. And when that reading failed to change her mind, she went through a third time, poring over one word at a time, trying to find double-meanings, mistaken identities, or unclear motivations.

"Now you see why I needed to show you, not just tell you?" Carl asked. His voice was soft and compassionate. She had already pieced the puzzle together, no doubt.

"I can't believe it was him all along."

"Old man is a blasted good actor; I'll give him that much," Carl replied. "He never ... you know ... tried anything, did he? I mean, you shared quarters and all."

Esper gave a sad, halfhearted smirk. "I made him turn away when I changed, and he never tried so much as a peek. You never would have known he was a grown man inside there. What are we going to do?"

"Well, we're certainly not letting him run loose," Carl said. "We locked him up in the escape pod. And we certainly can't deliver him to some poor, unsuspecting couple on Mars."

"You're not going to kill him, are you?" Esper asked, seeing where this line of logic was headed.

Carl scratched at the side of his head, losing his fingers in the mop of helmet-sweated hair. "Well, you see, we talked that one over, and none of us can kill a kid, even if he's not really a kid."

"So what, then?"

"We're turning him over to Harmony Bay," Carl replied.

Esper gasped. "But they'll—"

"Yeah, probably," Carl said, not even letting her finish. "But if we don't, and they get wind we had him, they'll dissect our brains to figure out where he went. We give him back; we wipe our hands clean of it. Tanny's already put the call in. They had a ship not too far off, be here in a few hours on a deep run."

Esper swallowed. There was a detail that Carl's plan was overlooking. "But they'll want me, too."

"That's why we have to kill you first."

Roddy sat on the floor of the cargo bay with a portable power supply and a multitool, all four hands working inside a panel of the escape pod. While the laaku worked, Adam knelt on one of the pod's seats, glaring out one of the windows. If looks could kill, his would have, but those sorts of powers were the province of wizards, not scientists. Without the tools of their various trades, men of science were just animals, left to the defenses of tooth and limb ... or voice, if they were lucky enough to find an adversary who could be overcome by reason or threat.

"That ought to do it," Roddy reported.

"Hey, Adam," Carl called out. "Can you hear me in there?"

"Let me out of here," Adam whined. "This isn't funny."

"You're not supposed to find it funny, Doctor Cliffton," Carl said, walking over to stand face to face with Adam, with just the window separating them. "None of *us* are laughing out here. You've left a lot of men dead in your trail and gotten their blood on our hands. But we've found you out."

"What do you mean? I'm not Doctor Cliffton; he's *old*. My name is Adam. It's Sister Theresa who's trying to get rid of you. She made me promise not to tell; she said she'd send me back to the Harmony Bay people if I didn't go along with her. I'm sorry. Please don't kill me."

Carl offered a reassuring smile. "Don't worry; we're not going to kill you. You're valuable. Your accomplice, on the other hand ..." Carl pointed outside Adam's field of view, and Tanny brought Esper over, wrists bound behind her back in a pair of duramite shackles they had found aboard the *Viper*. Though of similar heights, the difference in build between the two women was apparent in the ease with which Tanny manhandled the disgraced priestess.

"Adam, tell them I had nothing to do with this!" Esper pleaded, twisting around to face the escape pod. "Doctor Cliffton, don't let them kill me!" Carl had considered letting Esper think they were really going to go through with it, but he couldn't bring himself to be so cruel. Her acting was believable at least. It didn't hurt that Tanny had told her to give her best effort at breaking free. That much wasn't an act.

Within the escape pod, Adam grew quiet. "What do you want? I've got money, friends. I can get you things."

"If I believed a word of your promises I might consider it," Carl replied. "But considering you've tried at least twice to kill us, I'll take the bounty from Harmony Bay instead."

"Adam, *please!*" Esper shouted. Tanny forced her head down as she pushed Esper through the boarding tunnel. A moment later there was the thump of a door closing, and only Tanny returned.

"You're bluffing," Adam replied. "You aren't that cold blooded."

Carl put on his EV helmet, and then the rest of his suit. In full view of the escape pod, Roddy did likewise, and Tanny left for the common room. A klaxon sounded as the air was pumped from the cargo hold, quieting when no air was left to carry the sound. With Adam watching, Roddy cut the *Viper* free of the *Mobius*. Through careful maneuvering, the *Viper* stayed in view through the hole in the cargo bay door. Bolts of violet plasma from the *Mobius's* turret slammed into the drifting ship, carving holes in the hull until one ignited the ship's oxygen in a jet of flame. Several more shots and the *Viper* headed for the atmosphere of Delos IX.

Roddy began welding a plate in place to seal the cargo door.

"Show's over," Carl said through the comm in his helmet. Reaching down, he ripped the external power supply from the pod, ending communication with the furious and terrified occupant.

At the back of the cargo bay, outside the view of the escape pod, Esper stepped out of the personnel airlock in a poorly-fitted EV suit from the *Viper*. Carl held a finger to his lips, winked, and helped her up the stairs to the common room without tripping over boots five centimeters too big for her feet.

The *Bradbury* dropped from astral, gleaming in the light of the distant sun. It was no standard class that Carl was familiar with, but that wasn't surprising. The design was probably new since the last time he'd been in truly civilized space. Sleek and pristine white, it looked like a piece of medical equipment had been launched into space. Within seconds of arrival, the ship hailed them.

"*Vessel* Mobius, *this is the* Bradbury. *Hold position and prepare for docking.*" The voice was clear, crisp, and female, but whether it was human or computer, Carl couldn't tell.

"Friendly sorts," he muttered.

Tanny nodded and rolled her eyes, reaching for the comm. "*Bradbury*, this is *Mobius*, message confirmed. Holding position and releasing docking locks." She slumped back into the pilot's chair—her chair, Carl had to remind himself—and crossed her arms. "You feeling good about this?"

"Dumping the kid on them? Yeah," Carl said. "Because I can tell myself that if that ever really *was* a kid, the only ones who can get him back are the Harmony Bay scientists. If he was just a clone, and there's nothing more than an asshole scientist in there ... well, he's getting what's coming to him. Now ... if you meant whether I liked our odds of survival, I'm a coin-toss still."

Tanny grimaced. "That bad?"

Carl chuckled. "Naw, I think Mort'll pull us out of this just fine. You just stay up here, watch those instruments, and hit the throttle the second we're in astral. Oh ... and be careful, I had Roddy remove most of the safeties." Carl scurried from the cockpit before Tanny could retaliate against him.

Mort and Roddy were waiting for him in the cargo hold. Esper was hiding with Mriy in Mort's quarters. Carl had always been wary of the azrin around scientists, more for their safety than hers, and Esper obviously had to remain hidden. The spells in Mort's quarters ought to have been plenty to conceal them both.

The docking hatch opened in the center of the cargo hold floor, and a contingent of five climbed up one by one. The first two were security goons in pressed black uniforms that showed off bulging muscle beneath; they carried blaster pistols, but didn't look like the sorts who used them much. Next came a technician who juggled a scanner as she climbed the ladder into the *Mobius*. After her, an officer in a navy-style uniform, less the badges and rank insignia, scampered smartly up behind the technician; she was older, possibly close to Mort's age, with grey hair and an easy air of authority around her. Last came a hard-eyed man in an untucked shirt and denim pants.

"I am Captain Yasmira Dominguez of the *Bradbury*," the officer greeted them.

"Carl Ramsey," he replied, holding out his hand. "*Mobius* is my boat." To his surprise Captain Dominguez not only took the offered hand, but gave him a firm shake. It was the most respect he'd gotten out of anyone on as official a ship as the *Bradbury*. Maybe the corporate types weren't as bad as he gave them credit for.

"Where is the boy?" Captain Dominguez asked.

Carl pointed to Roddy, who flipped down a pair of protective goggles and flicked on a plasma torch. In seconds, he cut through the weld that sealed the pod shut. The two goons didn't need telling, they marched forward in lock step; one yanked open the door, the other grabbed Adam around the waist and hauled him out.

"Is this him?" Captain Dominguez asked. The tech and the hard-eyed man came forward; the tech fiddling with her scanner, the hard-eyed man staring at Adam intently.

"James," the hard-eyed man said. "If that's you in there, you'd better explain yourself. You're a crowning success if you are. If not, the team's prepped and ready for when we get you back; they'll figure out what's in that skull of yours."

Adam could not have looked more undignified without serious effort. He was slung beneath the arm of one of the goons, arms and legs dangling, squirming ineffectively. "Call them off, Alvin. Call them off. I'll show you everything."

"Where is your accomplice?" Captain Dominguez asked. "Where is Sister Theresa?"

"No one said anything about wanting her back," Carl put in. "We sent her down with the ship your friend here called in to dust us."

"She's dead?" Captain Dominguez asked. "You people executed her?"

"If you want to get technical," Carl replied. "We *told* her not to go into the *Viper*. But she didn't listen, and we cut it loose with her inside." It was a lie to cover a different lie, and Carl made no effort to sound sincere.

"Alvin, these people are monsters," Adam said. "If they didn't think they could get paid for returning me, they'd have sent me right along with her. Don't give them a single terra."

"We don't want any money," Carl said. Everyone stopped a moment to look at him like a zoo exhibit. "All I want is a guarantee that this little shit never bothers any of us again."

The lips of the man called Alvin twitched. "Oh, no worries of that." That sealed it; the *Bradbury* was going to dust them. Alvin lied like a ... well, like the ten-year-old Adam appeared to be. He probably thought he was being clever and coy.

"Well, we won't keep you any longer," Carl said. "We've got an appointment in the Orion cluster. We'll be heading out just as soon as you drop astral."

Carl waved as the delegation from the *Bradbury* climbed down to their own ship. As soon as the docking hatch closed, he sprinted up the steps to the common room and shouted to the wizard. "Get us astral now, and get us *deep*."

Carl ran to the cockpit as Mort chanted the spell to send them between stars. He was panting as he came up behind Tanny and looked at the displays. "They're just disengaging now," she reported.

Carl nodded. "Mort's ... got this." He hoped Mort had it.

He lost sight of the *Bradbury* through the cockpit windows and turned his attention to the radar, focusing on the distance between them and the Harmony Bay ship. They were still in the sensor shadow of Delos IX, hidden from view by the observation posts on Delos. In areas of unobserved space, there was no law, no rule, no witness. The *Bradbury* backed away to a safe range to blast them to dust.

An indicator light perked up, showing the *Bradbury* powering its plasma cannons. Tanny's finger was already over the button to raise their own shields. But before she even had to hit it, space dropped away around them. Delos IX took on a ghostly aspect, no longer green, but a wispy grey monochrome. The *Bradbury* was gone.

Tanny reached for the throttle, and they sped from the scene at a speed that the *Bradbury* couldn't hope to match. They didn't have Mordecai The Brown to send them 11.42 standard astral units deep.

Esper sat in the middle of Chip's old quarters, surrounded by boxes of his things. Despite the clutter, the room felt empty. The walls had been stripped bare of pictures. The floor was no longer supplemental storage for half the ship's communications systems. Chip's clothes were folded neatly inside a footlocker, along with a few datapads, a stack of Battle Minions datacards, and a thread-bare plush elephant. Carl had repatriated Chip's private stash of booze to the common area fridge, but the rest was bound for Mars and Chip's family, to be shipped at the next stop the *Mobius* made. Carl hadn't said yet where that would be.

With her hands folded in her lap, she found herself with nothing to do. The window view out into the astral void showed pinpricks of distant stars, barely drifting but passing at a phenomenal rate. It was all out there—all of it. The good, the bad, the in-between, and in all of it, nowhere to go. Maybe she would take Mort's advice and become a Seeker. She certainly hadn't found any answers yet, not to anything important. Going back to the One Church seemed ... unwise. Harmony Bay had likely reported her dead, if not to the proper authorities, then at least to the Church on Bentus VIII. Going back to her family was out of the question. Maybe some of her friends had broken free of the insidious grasp of New Singapore high society and left Mars for a simpler life.

Whatever she decided to do, it wouldn't be resolved sitting amid all Chip's belongings, fretting over it. Taking a deep, soul-cleansing breath, she resolved to park herself in front of the ship's holovid and wait to see where Carl decided to drop her off. She marched up the steps to find out what everyone was watching.

"Hey," Mort greeted her with a smile. His feet were up on the couch beside him, and he had a can of beer in hand. Roddy and Mriy acknowledged her as well, as they sat watching an old episode of Springwillow Valley. It just figured that of all the things they'd pick to watch, they chose a program she knew by heart. Mort reached over and grabbed another can. "Want one?" he asked.

Esper was about to refuse his offer by reflex, but instead paused to consider. She decided that she didn't want a beer, but she really *wanted* to want one. It had been years since the last time she was drunk, or even had anything more than a sip of wine. "Thanks, I think I will." She panicked when Mort threw it to her, holding out her hands in an awkward cross between a cradling motion and snatching something hot from a stove top. But the can stopped in mid-air, within easy reach. Before she could get mad at Mort for the prank, he smiled—it hadn't been a prank at all; it was just Mort's way of dealing with the world.

Esper popped the top and tipped it back. It was swill; the cheapest, hoppiest sewer water Earth exported: Earth's Preferred. She fought down the mouthful and gasped. Her mouth and throat burned. At Mort, Roddy, and Mriy's looks of concern, she offered a weak smile. "Before I came here, I hadn't had beer since I was ..." she fought to remember back, "... sixteen."

"When you think you can manage, Carl wanted to see you down in the cargo hold," Mort said.

"Oh?" she asked. "Did he say why?"

"Nope." The wizard's attention was clearly more focused on the soppy drama on the holovid than on whatever Carl was up to.

"Thanks," she replied. So instead of finding a place among the holovid viewers, she wove her way past them on her way to the cargo hold, jostling Mriy, who deigned not to say anything. Esper muttered an apology anyway.

She felt silly carrying a can of beer with her, but she didn't want to offend anyone by abandoning it with just a single sip gone. As she put her hand on the door, she heard strange, muffled music coming from the other side. When she opened the door, it hit her like an avalanche. Carl sat on the crate of expensive military guns, the ones they had taken from the first men Adam had hired to steal him away. He was playing the top half of a double-guitar, but it sounded broken. There was interference on the built-in speakers, making everything sound fuzzy and scratchy. It was a tune Esper had never heard before, and she had obviously come in the middle of it, because Carl kept playing after noticing her. He just gave her a quick nod, then lost himself in the music again. A few times she caught him wincing at an off-key note, but the whole thing sounded a bit off to her ears anyway. At the end, she gave an awkward clap around the can in her hand.

"I didn't know you were a musician," Esper said, coming down the steps to talk at a more comfortable distance.

"Not much of one," Carl replied, lifting the guitar strap over his head and resting the instrument by his feet. "This is Roddy's. He can play both sets at once. He'd have been a musician if he wasn't such a good mechanic."

"You should get it fixed if you're going to play it so loud," Esper said.

Carl chuckled and reached for a half-empty beer by his feet.

"It's not broken, that's just my playing. It's old classical rock music. My parents raised me on this shit. It seeped in. But that's not why I called you down here."

"Why did you?" Esper felt herself sweating, even though the environmental controls were working just fine.

"You give any thought to where you want to go, now that you're done with Adam?"

She had been right, it was time for *that* talk. "Some. But I had just figured I'd get off wherever you put down next. You're not a shuttle service, and I don't have money to hire you anyway."

"You give any thought to staying?"

"You mean ..."

"Yeah, once we ship Chip's things off to his folks, those can be your quarters, not just a borrowed bunk. And you wouldn't be stuck with a ten-year-old roommate."

"But what would I do around here? I'm not exactly crew material."

"It's not a matter of what you do," said Carl. "It's who you are. Have a seat and quit looking so nervous. Listen, you saved my life. I—"

"I didn't," Esper replied. "If Tanny had gotten back with the med kit first, you'd still have been fine."

"Maybe she would have saved my life if you didn't, but you did, not her," said Carl. He took a long chugging drink. "That counts for something around here. That makes you family. And I already know a secret that you need kept."

"Now, wait a minute," Esper said. The can in her hand made a metallic crinkling noise as she tightened her grip on it. "Don't think you can blackmail me into working for you!"

"Working for me?" Carl asked. "Maybe you haven't noticed, but no one around here seems to work for me. We just pitch in and keep this boat floating. I mention secrets because everyone has them. Some ugly ones, too. I don't care what you've done out there." Carl waved his beer in the vague direction of the universe. "But I know that the One Church thinks you're dead, and they've got to keep thinking that for your own good. If I didn't know that, I couldn't do anything to protect you from them. Same goes for Mort, for Tanny, for Roddy, and for Mriy. You saved my life, so I'll do the same for you."

"You have secrets, too, or are you just their keeper?" Esper asked.

Carl gave a rueful smile. "Tons. The most obvious one is that I'm an unrepentant liar."

Esper frowned. "Everyone knows that."

"Everyone *here* knows that," Carl corrected her. "But if you join the crew, I swear I'll *never* lie to you."

She stabbed an accusing finger at him. "That ... right there. That was a lie."

The cargo hold echoed with Carl's laughter. "And you see? That's why I'd take you on. You're quick. You can learn."

Esper still wasn't sure. It sounded like a scam. That was Carl's stock in trade, by his own admission. "But I'm not—"

"You're not what?" Carl cut her off. "You're not a priestess. You went to them looking for answers, but did you find them? No, they stuck you in front of a bunch of ten-year-olds to teach them long division."

"I taught fourth-grade algebra," Esper corrected him, but Carl kept barreling on. He was truly something to behold as an orator.

"You're not a spoiled rich girl, at least not anymore," he said. "The universe had a crazy notion to give you all the money in the world and an insane mother."

Esper's eyes went wide. "Mort said he wouldn't tell!"

Carl waved her objection away. "Tanny and I figured it out your first day on board. She pegged it that your mother was a doll collector, and thought you should look like one, too."

"I never thought of it like that ..."

"I don't know what you are, frankly," Carl said. "You're like new clay, still able to be anything."

"What if I'm not good at anything?"

"You think Tanny's the best pilot I could find? You think I like my mechanic being drunk off his ass eighteen hours a day and sleeping the other six? You think I need a bodyguard who sleeps the eighteen?"

"Or a wizard who can ruin your ship?"

"It's a bit different with Mort," Carl said. "He was friends with my parents. I wouldn't trade him for ten wizards just as good."

"I'll agree, under one condition," said Esper.

"What's that?" Carl took a sip of his beer and waited.

"You tell me the *real* reason you want me on your crew."

Carl was silent for a moment. He set his drink on the floor and leaned back with a thoughtful expression on his face. "All right ... no bullshit. You need us. Same way the rest of us need each other. They don't know it yet, but they'll need you, too. I already needed you; you saved my life. This is sort of a roving colony of misfits and outcasts."

Esper huffed, unsure whether to follow though. It *sounded* like a bull-poo answer ... no, it sounded like bullshit. But it made sense, too, in a Carlish sort of way. A chance to make herself over. A chance to start fresh, with people who had some idea where she had been and didn't hold it against her. A chance to fit in.

"What do I need to sign?"

"Nothing," said Carl. "You're in. We don't have a lot of rules around here. No one goes in anyone else's quarters without their say-so. Most of us waive that, but Tanny's not allowed in mine and vice versa. When we get a paying job, the split goes even to each of us, including *Mobius*."

"The ship gets a share?"

"Pays for fuel, repairs, upgrades ... yeah, he gets a share. And before you ask, *Mobius* is a 'he.' I was originally going to name him Star Ghost, but Mort made a better case. Way he put it, a mobius loop only has one side, so there's no place to be *but* all on the same side. And no matter how far you travel on it, you'll eventually come back."

"How often do you come full circle?" Esper asked, still smirking at the thought of a ship named Star Ghost. It was something one of her students might have come up with.

"I'll let you know the first time it happens," Carl replied. "Next place we stop, instead of leaving you there we'll get you your own EV suit, so you won't have to flop around in one that doesn't fit." He glanced at the can clutched in Esper's hand. "Oh, and there's one other rule around here."

"What's that?"

"We don't waste beer. Bottoms up."

Ready for book 2? *A Smuggler's Conscience* is available for you right now. Continue reading for an excerpt.

PREVIEW: A SMUGGLER'S CONSCIENCE
BLACK OCEAN: GALAXY OUTLAWS MISSION 2

The job: a delivery, no questions asked. The problem: curiosity is a deadly sin.

A simple pickup and delivery. No questions asked; no looking inside the cargo. All it requires is a fast, stealthy ship and a crew who can keep their imaginations and consciences in check until the drop-off. The *Mobius* is up to the task, but when the crew can't control their curiosity, they're faced with a moral dilemma. Do they cut their losses? Contact the authorities? Take the money and run?

Or do they get talked into the stupidest, most reckless, and least profitable course of action they could possibly take? Doing the right thing.

WITH AN IMPACT that drove the breath from her lungs, the cargo bay stopped spinning around Esper. An uncomfortable pressure released from her shoulder socket, and her arm slapped limply to the mat. Overheard lights shone down into her eyes, forcing her to close them. She heard footsteps, and a shadow passed over her; a hand grabbed hers and hauled her to her feet.

"You try scratching me in the face again, I'll dump you even harder," Tanny said.

Esper slumped forward, hands braced against her knees as she caught her breath. Tanny was dripping with sweat, but otherwise seemed unbothered by the exertion of throwing her around. "Sorry," she replied. "It's an old habit. I never got into fights as a schoolteacher. I mostly just broke them up."

"It shows," Tanny said, putting her hands on her hips. She wore padded fingerless gloves and a padded helmet, along with aerobic workout gear and bare feet. Esper was unprotected, but trusted Tanny not to actually *hit* her. "You fight like a little girl. I'm guessing you only had sisters."

"Nope," Esper replied between breaths. "Two older brothers. Never laid a hand on me."

"Must have been a lot older."

"Eight and twelve years," said Esper. She took one huge breath and forced herself upright.

Tanny nodded. "Usually it's the only children who never learn how to fight, or the ones who grew up in space aboard ship. Spend enough time around kids your own age, you learn how."

"I'm not sure I'm cut out to be a marine," Esper said.

Tanny cracked her knuckles and settled into a defensive stance. "Well, no shit. This isn't about making you into a boxer; it's about keeping you from being a liability." Esper threw a punch, but Tanny caught her by the wrist. Poking a finger inside Esper's fist, Tanny popped her thumb out. "You'll break your thumb if you hit someone like that. And use an open palm trying for my jaw. You'd bruise your knuckles if you hit someone like that."

"You didn't care about me being a liability when I was a passenger," Esper pointed out. She bounced on the balls of her feet like Tanny had shown her and threw another punch, which Tanny batted aside.

"I'd written you off. I knew if anything happened, I'd have to save you," Tanny replied, throwing a slow punch meant to force Esper to duck out of the way. "Now that you're part of the crew, it would be nice if you weren't such a pushover. It's bad enough how often I had to bail out Carl or Chip."

"I thought Carl was in the navy," Esper said. She swung her foot around in a clumsy kick that Tanny accepted to the side with a grunt, not even bothering to defend herself. "Shouldn't he have learned all this stuff?"

"Navy and tough don't belong in the same sentence; at least not without an 'ain't' thrown in somewhere," Tanny said. "Carl was the biggest wimp on board until you showed up."

Esper pulled up short, taking a tap on the cheek from Tanny's gloved right fist for her lapse. "Even Roddy? I mean he's so—"

"Stronger than he looks, and quicker, too," Tanny finished for her. "Chip wasn't much better, but he was ten years younger." Tanny's expression went flat for a moment, and her shoulders slumped. "Anyway, me and Mriy are the ones who keep everyone safe planetside."

"You had all this equipment on board," Esper noted, pointing to the protective padding Tanny wore. "Do you and her fight like this?"

Tanny laughed. "I could maybe take her in a points-only boxing match, but marine conditioning can't make up for azrin physiology and a lifetime of hunting her own meals."

Esper sighed and stepped back off the edge of the mat, the cold steel of the cargo hold floor icy against her bare feet. "It just makes me wonder what I've gotten myself into. I mean, Carl said

I'd find a way to fit in, but I just don't see anything I can do that you need."

"This really isn't a ship," Tanny replied. "This is an asylum where the patients all pitch in to fly."

Carl and Mort sat on the couch with Roddy as the laaku introduced them to one of his species' greatest cultural exports—the action holovid. While human audiences had tended to move either up or way, way down the scale of sophisticated entertainment, the laaku people had been turning out the best unapologetic, mind-numbing adrenaline pumpers for decades. Carl had seen real-life laaku fight—even Roddy once or twice—but it looked nothing like the physics-defying acrobatics filling the holovid field. Quadridexterous bare-fisted masters were slugging it out with some sort of demons taken from the mythology of a lost sub-division of the laaku species. The battle was playing out at a temple perched on the edge of a smoke-belching volcano, giving Carl a hint as to why this particular people might have died out.

When the door to the cargo bay opened, all heads in the room turned to look. Tanny and Esper stumbled through, their workout clothes and hair soaked with sweat. Carl looked from Tanny and her glistening bare arms to Esper with her shirt plastered against her skin, then back again. Without taking his eyes from them, he leaned close to Roddy. "Think you could install some security cameras in the hold? I think we've been watching the wrong feed."

Roddy made a rude, flapping noise with his lips. "Face it; you blew all your chances with Tanny. She's probably warned Esper off by now, too."

"Whatever they were doing down there's still better holo than what's on now," Carl replied.

"What are you kiddies whispering about over there?" Tanny asked, inclining her head in Carl and Roddy's general direction. She grabbed a can of ReCharge from the fridge and cracked it open, then offered a second can to Esper.

Esper's face was flushed from exertion, but the redness deepened and she turned and whispered something to Tanny.

"No shit," Tanny replied loudly enough for everyone to hear. "I just want them to cop to it. I don't care if you watch us or not, but I catch any cameras in the shower or my quarters, I'm airlocking you ... both of you." She added a pointed look in Roddy's direction. It wasn't as if Carl was likely to manage any modifications to the ship without the laaku's help.

"The humors spilleth over," Mort said with a chuckle. "Been cooped up too long in this little box. When we get planetside, take care of yourselves, the lot of you."

"Yeah," Tanny replied. "Whenever *that* might be. We've been floating aimlessly for five days. Be nice if our *captain* would do some captaining and get us some work."

"I'm working ..." Carl replied with an easy smile. His statement at odds with lounging on the couch with his feet on the base of the holovid.

"Yeah, bullsh—" Tanny said.

"He found something," Esper interrupted, perking up. "Didn't you?"

Carl pointed a limp finger in Esper's direction. "Give that lady a cashier's chit. Yeah, I'm waiting to hear back from a guy, but we're headed his way."

"What guy?" Tanny asked, her brow furrowing. She took a long swig of ReCharge as she waited for his reply.

"Well, technically not a 'guy' guy, but she's—"

Tanny spluttered, spitting half a mouthful back into the can. "Not that creepy old bitch!"

"Lay off. She's fine. And she pays," Carl replied. "Mriy's already punched in the heading, just in case."

"You let Mriy—"

"Mriy can work the nav computer," Carl snapped. "It's not yours. Roddy can work it, too. Hell, even I know how to use it. Mort's the only one on board who ..." Carl turned to Esper. "You know how to plot a course in the navcom?"

Esper shrank back from the sudden attention. She shrugged.

"Everyone but Mort and Esper can work it," Carl said.

"Fine," Tanny replied. "But you can go meet her by yourself. Or just take Mort; she likes *him* well enough."

Mort cleared his throat. "Not this time. I've got something to look into when we set down."

"Since when have you got business?" Roddy asked. "Not that it's any of mine."

"Whose business is any of this?" Esper asked. "Who is this mystery person you might be meeting?"

A few notes from an ancient song chimed from Carl's datapad. "Speak of the devil," he said. "This is her." He turned the datapad in Esper's direction as he hurried to his quarters.

The name on the screen read: Keesha Bell.

Grab a copy of *A Smuggler's Conscience*, book 2 of *Black Ocean: Galaxy Outlaws*, and continue your adventure now.

BOOKS BY J. S. MORIN

Black Ocean

Black Ocean is a vivid 26th century story universe where science and magic coexist—sort of.

Black Ocean: Galaxy Outlaws

Black Ocean: Galaxy Outlaws is a fast-paced fantasy space opera series about the small crew of the *Mobius* trying to squeeze out a living. If you love fantasy and sci-fi, and still lament over the cancellation of *Firefly*, *Black Ocean: Galaxy Outlaws* is the series for you.

Read about the *Black Ocean: Galaxy Outlaws* series and discover where to buy at: galaxyoutlawsmissions.com

Black Ocean: Astral Prime

Co-written with author M.A. Larkin, *Black Ocean: Astral Prime* hearkens back to location-based space sci-fi classics like *Babylon 5* and *Star Trek: Deep Space Nine*. *Astral Prime* builds on the rich *Black Ocean* universe, introducing a colorful cast of characters for new and returning readers alike. Come along for the ride as a minor outpost in the middle of nowhere becomes a key point of interstellar conflict.

Read about the *Black Ocean: Astral Prime* series and discover where to buy at: astralprimemissions.com

Black Ocean: Mercy for Hire

Black Ocean: Mercy for Hire follows the exploits of a pair of do-gooder bounty hunters who care more about saving the day than securing a payday. The series builds on the rich *Black Ocean* universe, centering on a couple of fan-favorites and introducing a colorful cast for new and returning readers alike. Fans of vigilante justice and heroes who exemplify the word will love this series.

Read about *Black Ocean: Mercy for Hire* and discover where to buy at: mercyforhiremissions.com

Black Ocean: Mirth & Mayhem

Black Ocean: Mirth & Mayhem delves into the origins of two vagabonds making their living among the stars. Mort is a wizard coming to grips with a life on the run and estrangement from the comforts and respect he had on Earth. Brad is an impressionable youth, too clever for his—or anyone's—good. And Chuck Ramsey is the mold that Brad's trying to break out of, which is harder than he could ever have dreamed.

Read about *Black Ocean: Mirth & Mayhem* and discover where to buy at: mirthandmayhemmissions.com

Black Ocean: Passage of Time

The year was 2586. A few minutes later, it was 2591. Caught up in a time travel snafu, Eric and Jessie Ramsey become fugitives from the people who want answers as to how they did it —and where their loyalties lie in the galactic war that broke out in their absence.

Read about *Black Ocean: Passage of Time* and discover where to buy at: passageoftimemissions.com

Twinborn Chronicles

The *Twinborn Chronicles* is an epic fantasy saga based on the possibility that our dreams offer us a glimpse into the life of another – another who can get the same glimpse into our world. Read about the *Twinborn Chronicles* and discover where to buy at: twinbornchronicles.com

Twinborn Chronicles: Awakening

Experience the journey of mundane scribe Kyrus Hinterdale who discovers what it means to be Twinborn—and the dangers of getting caught using magic in a world that thinks it exists only in children's stories.

Twinborn Chronicles: War of 3 Worlds

Then continue on into the world of Korr, where the Mad Tinker and his daughter try to save the humans from the oppressive race of Kuduks. When their war spills over into both Tellurak and Veydrus, what alliances will they need to forge to make sure the right side wins?

Project Transhuman

Project Transhuman brings genetic engineering into a postapocalyptic Earth, 1000 years aliens obliterated all life.

These days, even the humans are built by robots.

Charlie7 is the oldest robot alive. He's seen everything from the fall of mankind at the hands of alien invaders to the rebuilding of a living world from the algae up. But what he hasn't seen in over a thousand years is a healthy, intelligent human. When Eve stumbles into his life, the old robot finally has something worth coming out of retirement for: someone to protect.

Read about all of the *Project Transhuman* books and discover where to buy at: projecttranshuman.com

Sins of Angels

Co-written with author M.A. Larkin, *Sins of Angels* is an epic space opera series set 3000 years after the fall of Earth. With the scope of *Dune* and the adventurous spirit of *Indiana Jones*, it delivers a conflict that spans galaxies and rests on the spirit of brave researcher Professor Rachel Jordan. Follow the complete saga, and watch as the fate of our species hangs in the balance.

Read about *Sins of Angels* and discover where to buy at: sinsofangelsbooks.com

Shadowblood Heir

Shadowblood Heir explores what would happen if the writer of your favorite epic fantasy TV show died before the show ended—and the show was responsible. If you wonder what it would be like if an epic fantasy world invaded our world, this urban fantasy story might give you that glimpse.

Read about *Shadowblood Heir* and discover where to buy at: shadowbloodheir.com

EMAIL INSIDERS

You made it to the end! Maybe you're just persistent, but hopefully that means you enjoyed the book. But this is just the end of one story. If you'd like reading my books, there are always more on the way!

Perks of being an Email Insider include:

- Notification of book releases (often with discounts)
- Inside track on beta reading
- Advance review copies (ARCs)
- Access to Inside Exclusive bonus extras and giveaways
- Best of my blog about fantasy, science fiction, and the art of worldbuilding

Sign up for the my Email Insiders list at: jsmorin.com/updates

ABOUT THE AUTHOR

I am a creator of worlds and a destroyer of words. As a fantasy writer, my works range from traditional epics to futuristic fantasy with starships. I have worked as an unpaid Little League pitcher, a cashier, a student library aide, a factory grunt, a cubicle drone, and an engineer—there is some overlap in the last two.

Through it all, though, I was always a storyteller. Eventually I started writing books based on the stray stories in my head, and people kept telling me to write more of them. Now, that's all I do for a living.

I enjoy strategy, worldbuilding, and the fantasy author's privilege to make up words. I am a gamer, a joker, and a thinker of sideways thoughts. But I don't dance, can't sing, and my best artistic efforts fall short of your average notebook doodle. When you read my books, you are seeing me at my best.

My ultimate goal is to be both clever and right at the same time. I have it on good authority that I have yet to achieve it.

Connect with me online
jsmorin.com

facebook.com/authorjsmorin

twitter.com/authorjsmorin

bookbub.com/authors/j-s-morin

goodreads.com/JSMorin

tiktok.com/@authorjsmorin